LOVE
ON A
TWO-WAY STREET

Also by JL King

Pocket Books / Karen Hunter Publishing
New York London Toronto Sydney

LOVE
ON A
TWO-WAY STREET

By JL King and
Tremell McKenzie

Pocket Books
A Division of Simon & Schuster, Inc.
1230 Avenue of the Americas
New York, NY 10020

Karen Hunter Publishing
A Division of Suitt-Hunter Enterprises, LLC
598 Broadway, 3rd Floor
New York, NY 10012

First Karen Hunter Publishing/Pocket Books trade paperback edition July 2009

POCKET and colophon are registered trademarks of Simon & Schuster, Inc.

For information about special discounts for bulk purchases, please contact Simon & Schuster Special Sales at 1-866-506-1949 or business@simonandschuster.com.

The Simon & Schuster Speakers Bureau can bring authors to your live event. For more information or to book an event contact the Simon & Schuster Speakers Bureau at 1-866-248-3049 or visit our website at www.simonspeakers.com.

Designed by Jamie Kerner-Scott

Manufactured in the United States of America

10 9 8 7 6 5 4 3 2 1

Library of Congress Cataloging-in-Publication Data for the hardcover edition is available.

ISBN 978-1-4165-6632-8

*This book is dedicated to every storyteller who
has a story inside of him that is dying to be told*

THE BEGINNING
Newark, New Jersey

Little James Lamar Kennedy lay, wide awake, on top of his wafer-thin twin mattress, wearing his dingy long johns that doubled as pajamas. He was still. The stench of smoke, old dirt, and roaches filled his home, but James was oblivious. He had long since tuned out the occasional sirens, the raised voices, and the stray dogs barking, fixtures in his surroundings.

On this night he was single-minded. He held his breath and could feel his little heart pounding against his bony chest. He was a thinking little boy. And tonight he was contemplating death. Not his own. Those nightmares about falling into a bottomless pit, or being chased by some unidentifiable, scary figure had long since subsided. James's reality was so much more horrifying.

Every night for the past few months a man had come into

his room and done to him the unthinkable. He hurt James, the scrawny nine-year-old with bright eyes and a determined spirit. But the pain wasn't located in a place James could identify. It wasn't so much physical, in his stomach or in his head, or even in his joints. This pain was deeper, much deeper. And it made him feel bad all the time.

James hurt deep inside his soul—not that he could even imagine what a soul was at his age. But what he knew was that the pain made him nauseous and he wanted it to stop. When nighttime came, James would lie still, eyes open, waiting, all of his muscles tensed, his stomach in a complete knot. He waited for his reality bogeyman to come. He waited for the man his mother told him to call Uncle Benny.

On the few nights Uncle Benny didn't come, James still couldn't sleep because he never knew *if* he would come. There wasn't a set time for Uncle Benny to come into little James's room, climb on top of him, and press James's small face, almost to the point of suffocation, into his old foam pillow. He would come when he felt like coming. And before, during, and after, James wanted to die.

On this night, however, James wanted to kill.

"If you say anything, boy, I will kill you, your mother, and everybody else up in this bitch!" Uncle Benny would whisper, his breath putrid, before leaving James's room.

But James did tell. He told the only person he could trust. And together they hatched a plan. Andre Bonner, three years older than James, was twelve but already six feet tall and muscular. He wasn't just big for his age, he could be brutal—a characteristic he'd developed in order to survive. There was no daddy or big brother around to protect Andre, or Bones, as he would be called. He learned early on that he would have to protect himself and was known on the streets as a fighter. In school, he was a bully. But for little James, he was a savior. Bones and James told everyone they were cousins. The two had distinctly different personalities—James was more outgoing and charming, and was always joking, his way of trying to get classmates to look past his funky, dirty clothes, and bugged-out mother. Bones was serious and quiet, not giving a damn about what others thought.

Their mothers were best friends, or, more accurately, running buddies. Tawana, Bones's mother, and Deidre, James's mother, did everything together. Everything. When James's father had been stabbed to death outside a Central Ward, Newark, New Jersey, pool hall when James was just five, the two women got apartments right next to each other in the New Hope Projects. And the two "sisters" began smoking crack together.

While their mothers walked the streets looking for ways to get their next fix, Bones looked after James. He was his baby-sitter and only friend. When James had any problems, like being teased at school for his unkempt appearance, he would threaten, "I'm going to get my cousin Bones to come here and kick your ass!" And Bones would come. He would always come.

Bones wasn't there on the nights Uncle Benny visited. He was in his own run-down apartment, dealing with his own demons as his mother was getting high. Bones was there for James on this night, though, hiding quietly on the floor, beside James's bed. He couldn't be seen from the door. He had promised little James that he would take care of his visitor. Bones had a brick, wrapped in a pillowcase, by his side.

The gaunt man sneaked into James's room, careful to lock the door behind him. Every muscle in James's little body tightened.

"Boy, you know what you're supposed to do," the man whispered through clenched teeth. "Turn over and pull those pants down!"

As the man swiftly worked to undo the zipper of his own pants and climb on top of James, Bones sprang into action. He swung his brick-filled pillowcase like a slingshot and the load landed in the back of Benny's head. The frail-looking man, although caught off guard, didn't go down. He started swinging his arms, his hands balled up in fists, in search of a target. Bones brought the heavy sack back to deliver another blow. The man struck Bones across the face with a punch, sending him reeling back into the bedroom wall.

James jumped on Benny's back, trying to dig out his eyes. This bought Bones enough time to recover. He took the brick out of the pillowcase and ran full force, brick in hand, and smashed it into the man's nose. He heard the horrifying sound of bones and cartilage being crushed. Benny buckled to his knees, covering his bleeding face with his hands. Bones then reached for a belt discarded on the floor, and wrapped it around the man's throat.

"Come on lil man, help me pull!" Bones called out to James, who stood frozen in the background of darkness.

With both feet lodged in the man's back, Bones pulled on the end of the belt with all his might. He tugged the belt with a strength he didn't know he had. He pulled as if his own life depended on it. He felt adrenaline course through his veins as the man's life slowly faded. The man was struggling and gurgling as the blood from his nose bubbled into the back of his throat.

Bones and James and the man were on the floor, tangled and heaving for seconds that seemed to tick away as slowly as hours. Finally the man's body went limp. Bones and James were sweating and out of breath.

"Is he, is he . . . dead?" James said, managing to break the silence.

"I think so," Bones said. "We have to get him out of here and clean up this mess."

In an ordinary home, with an ordinary mother, the ruckus alone would have caused someone to investigate. But this was not an ordinary home. It had yellowed walls, once project-issue white. The kitchen had little food, but still teemed with roaches so bold that neither light nor movement caused them to scatter. They openly walked around searching for crumbs or whatever else they could eat, just like the people who lived here. The bathroom hadn't been cleaned in months, the toilet filthier than a Porta Potti at a sporting event. This was a home inhabited by adults who no longer cared about much—except getting high. This was a crack den.

James's mother, Deidre, tired of going to the streets for her fixes, decided to open her home to her junkie buddies. She provided them with a hidden, safe place to get high. The price of admission? Crack. They got to smoke for as long as they wanted provided that they took care of the hostess. There were occasional fights once the crack ran out, fights primarily over who would go out and do whatever they had to do to bring more back. Deidre would try to keep the fights to a low simmer because she didn't want to bring the heat down on her situation. If Bones and James didn't clean up this mess, Deidre would have more heat than she could imagine.

The two boys struggled to drag Benny's crackhead body out of James's first-floor bedroom window. Quick-thinking Bones had stolen a couple of heavy-duty, extra-large garbage bags from the janitor's closet at his school.

"Let's get him in this bag," Bones said. "It'll be easier to drag him and we won't have to worry about leaving a trail of blood. We have enough to clean up after we get rid of him."

Benny didn't weigh much alive, but the dead weight was real. They managed to drag him out of the window and then into the back alley near the Dumpster. This was Newark, which despite its movement toward change with its downtown arena, baseball stadium, and acclaimed performing-arts center, was still, well, Newark. People were killed here just about every other day. This alleyway was dark, but they could see the shadows of trash bags overflowing the Dumpster. They were smelly and sticky and some weren't properly tied, but Bones and Juice had to move a few out of the middle of the large container to make enough space for Benny's body bag. They then piled the bags, dripping with all kinds of filth, on top of him.

"This will be our little secret," Bones said, brushing his hands together, trying to get the visible filth off. They were still sticky from the garbage bags and the blood.

The two climbed back in through the window. Bones took James's sheet and ripped it into rags. He went to the kitchen and found an old pot that hadn't been used in years, filled it with hot water, and came back and cleaned the room, ringing out the blood-filled rags and replacing the water five times. Everyone in the apartment was too busy to notice a thing.

"You can't tell anyone or else we'll both be in a lot of trouble, okay?" Bones said again, once they'd left the apartment, in search of a place to put the last pieces of evidence, making sure little James knew the ramifications of what they had just done.

"Okay," James said as they put the last of the bloody rags in the garbage can down the block. "Bones . . ."

"Yeah, lil man, what's up?" asked Bones, looking around to make sure nobody saw them.

"I'm going to be rich one day, and when I am, I'm going to take care of you."

Bones laughed. He had not laughed in such a long time that he surprised himself.

"I'm serious!" said James, insulted.

"I know you are, lil man, I know you are," Bones responded. "So how do you plan on becoming rich, because I don't know how much longer I can live like this."

"I don't know," James replied. "I just know that I will be. You'll see!"

Bones shook his head as the two boys walked back to their building. James entered his apartment while watching Bones close the door to his, next door. James's living room was dark except for the flicker of lighters that sparked through the room as if it was its own galaxy. There were heavy red curtains on the windows to protect this haven from possible outside prying eyes in the adjacent buildings. James carefully navigated the room to avoid bumping into anybody who might have been sitting on the floor.

"I saw Uncle Benny go into your room, but ain't seen him come out."

James walked faster as he recognized his mother's voice. Feeling her eyes follow him to his bedroom, he put his hand on the knob, then turned to see his mother sitting on a wobbly stool in the place where the couch had been. During one doping night she'd been offered ten dollars for it and had taken it.

"Benny owe me some money," said Deidre, mostly out of it.

The woman, who looked fifteen years older than she should have, had dry ashy lips and thick, unpermed hair that was standing up around her head as if she were some sort of wild Medusa.

James paid her no attention. She never had the energy to really pursue anything and he knew that if he just ignored her, she would go away. He went back into his room. He and Bones had done a good job of cleaning up. James, who even at this young age was a bit of a perfectionist, moved his little items, which had been knocked out of place during the struggle, back into their accustomed spots. When everything was back where it belonged, he lay on top of his sheetless bed.

It was the best night's sleep little James Lamar Kennedy had had in a while.

TWENTY-FIVE YEARS LATER
New York City

James Lamar Kennedy, known to the world as Juice because of the amount of influence he had in so many arenas, stood at the altar in his white silk Armani tuxedo, a stark contrast against his chocolate skin. He wore a white silk bow tie and the biggest diamond cuff links money could buy. Standing next to him in a black custom-made tuxedo with a white colored tie and shirt to match Juice's tux was Bones. His waves were shining in the sunlight coming through the church's giant stained-glass windows, his mustache and sideburns trimmed to perfection. Everything was perfect. The perfect flowers, the perfect best man, the perfect groom, and, of course, the perfect bride.

Juice stood there, daring a bead of sweat to form on his brow and ruin his cool. He was also trying to stop his stomach from flip-flopping. Nerves, something he hadn't felt in some time.

Juice had become a master at masking his feelings—or eliminating them altogether. Emotions were for weaklings, he believed. He put them on display only for effect when he was trying to manipulate someone into doing what he wanted. Even when he showed anger, it was only for a purpose.

Juice was the most powerful man in the music industry and secretly one of the most powerful men in the world. He'd gotten there on talent, yes, but more so through manipulation and Machiavellian tactics.

Fresh out of high school, Juice had begun as an intern; actually, there hadn't been an official position, unpaid or otherwise. He'd created it. He knew Universal Records was one of the biggies in the industry. So he'd shown up one day saying he had an appointment with the head of the black music department. Juice had done his homework; he knew everything about this man, right down to the kind of Starbucks coffee he drank.

While the assistant picked up the phone to see if this young man did indeed have an appointment, Juice rushed past the desk and into the office of Rick Roby.

"Mr. Roby, before you throw me out, I want you to know that you will not find a more dedicated, hardworking person to help you build your division into number one in the industry!"

Juice then rattled off each and every artist the label had signed and exactly what he thought was wrong and right about him or her.

"I'm sorry, sir!" The assistant came rushing behind Juice, out of breath. But it was too late. In a matter of seconds, Juice was able to impress Rick Roby enough to be given a chance.

"I like your style, kid," Rick Roby said, clearly charmed by Juice. "But don't you ever barge into my office like that again!"

Juice didn't have to. In just three months, he went from

being an intern whose primary job was getting Roby's Starbucks, to being Roby's assistant, doing everything from answering Roby's email to working with artists in the studio. Juice would often stay after a studio session was over. The department had already paid for the time and Juice took advantage, creating music and lyrics for new artists in his off-hours. He preferred to bestow his talents on unknown artists, people with the odds against them. He wanted to show that he could turn a sow's ear into a silk purse.

Juice made himself such an invaluable assistant that Roby started giving him more rope, allowing him to sell some of his beats. Juice took that rope and used it to lasso even more opportunities for himself, actually discovering new talent.

He found the unlikely stars in the most unlikely places. He turned a boy from Harlem with a speech impediment into the hottest rapper in the game. He found a girl who was once strung out on crack and transformed her into a hip-hop sensation.

Juice had a sixth sense about music. That gift put him in a position not just to rise through the ranks in the music business, but to take it over. Roby's boss began to see that the person bringing revenue to the company by finding new talent wasn't Roby, but his trusted assistant. And in the world of follow-the-money, Roby and his huge six-figure salary and expense account became expendable.

After securing his boss's job, Juice had his sights set on his own label. He found an ally in an unlikely place to help him realize that goal. The man was Mortimer Zane, billionaire real estate mogul. Juice got his record label and more.

On this day, the "more" included one of the hottest women in the world—or at least that's how *Maxim* magazine described her. She was not just hot, she was the kind of woman a man would want to take home to meet mama. Juice would never take her home to meet mama. But he *was* going to marry her.

He looked confidently out into the crowd, making eye contact with certain dignitaries, superstar athletes, actors, and business moguls. Missing from the more than three hundred invitees was Juice's mother. Billing himself as an orphan, he didn't want any reporters or paparazzi questioning or photographing her. He was not going to be embarrassed on his special day. The years of drug abuse had not been kind to Deidre and no amount of money could clean up that look.

Somewhere in New Jersey, though, Deidre was tuned into E!, which was broadcasting the wedding live. It was also being simulcast on BET, which even had a white-carpet special interviewing several of the guests before the wedding. This was the closest Deidre would get to her son—sitting in front of the fifty-inch plasma television that Juice's money had bought her, watching his wedding.

The camera panned to the full orchestra, led by a harpist who began to play for the procession of bridesmaids and ushers.

Outside, four white Bentley convertibles, two Mercedes Maybachs, and one white Phantom Rolls-Royce were lined up in front of Trinity Temple on what seemed to be a day made in heaven. Traffic flow had been altered for the union between the queen of pop and one of the most powerful men in the music industry.

When Juice met Brianna, it had been love at first note. The moment he heard her voice he knew she was a rare find. And she was the most beautiful songstress he had ever seen.

"It was supposed to rain today," said the driver of the Mercedes as he leaned discreetly against the open door of one of the Bentleys. "Damn, Juice must have paid off Mother Nature to make sure it wouldn't rain on his big day."

"Stick around, young blood," responded Woodrow Charles, the driver of the Rolls-Royce, Juice's personal car. "You ain't seen nothing yet! You won't believe the things this cat is controlling."

Woodrow had been Juice's driver for three years. He'd landed the job by accident one night when his dispatcher called for an emergency fill-in for the night. The driver Juice normally used had been fired that morning when he hadn't arrived exactly at 2:30 A.M. to pick Juice up at the studio. The former driver claimed he hadn't heard the alarm. Woodrow was there, and on time.

Woodrow took out a handkerchief and shined away a smudge that had somehow managed to make its way to the driver's-side window. He stood at attention, trying his best to look like one of those guards with the funny hats who camped out in front of Buckingham Palace.

Woodrow loved his job. Since signing on, he had become part baby-sitter, part bodyguard, part secret keeper, and part driver. He knew his role and he knew how to keep his mouth closed. In exchange, the pay was good—really good—for a high school dropout. Woodrow had gone from being a forty-one-year-old man selling weed on 135th Street and Malcolm X Boulevard, in a playground across the street from Harlem Hospital, to owning his own one-bedroom condo in Jersey City, New Jersey, and always having a pocket full of cash. It was nothing for Juice to throw Woodrow a few hundreds just because. And Woodrow had saved every hundred-dollar bill he'd gotten like that from Juice. It really added up.

There were other perks to being Juice's driver. Woodrow got to rub elbows with many of the biggest names in show business and business-business. He didn't actually rub elbows, but he did get to see many of them up close and some closer than he expected from his rearview mirror. Juice had a lot of juice and Woodrow loved being in the middle of it.

The mayor of New York City ordered that the street be shut down for five hours for the wedding procession. The city police department had set up barricades—similar to the ones used for parades and the New Year's Eve ball dropping in Times Square—across the street from the church. There were thousands of people pushing and jockeying for position with their digital cameras and camera phones in hand.

Woodrow winked at a girl who had a position near the front. She must have camped out overnight to get that spot. Woodrow remembered her from two years before when she had given Juice a blow job in the back of a Lincoln town car. She would show up anywhere and everywhere Juice was after that, hoping for a chance at a repeat performance. Juice rarely gave a groupie a second taste.

Woodrow watched the spectacle across the street grow with the crowd, while throngs of celebrities entered the church. In addition to the movie stars and music icons, there was a banking mogul, a television executive, an owner of an NBA team, and a senator who many believed could very well be the next president of the United States of America.

Musical selections from the harpist were piped outside the church, filling the streets with celestial sounds. When the Lohengrin's wedding march began, the crowd started to cheer in anticipation. While they couldn't see what was happening inside, their excitement made it feel as if the wedding was actually taking place on the streets.

Woodrow checked his watch. In Juice's normal fashion, the

wedding was being run as if it were a union-worked concert—like clockwork. It was noon and the bride would be making her way down the aisle. According to rehearsals, the rest of the ceremony should take no more than thirty minutes. Juice and Brianna, as man and wife, would greet the guests at the door and then Woodrow would have the car ready to roll to Tavern on the Green, which was rented out for the reception. The bridal party would have their pictures taken on the beautifully landscaped grounds. At five o'clock, Mr. and Mrs. James Lamar "Juice" Kennedy would leave for Teterboro Airport, where they would board Juice's private plane to an uncharted island in the Caribbean for their honeymoon—no paparazzi, no other tourists. It was said to be the most beautiful place on earth, a modern-day Garden of Eden. For ten days, Juice and Brianna would consummate their marriage and enjoy unimaginable pampered bliss. Juice had hired servants, chefs, and masseuses. He'd even hired Brianna's favorite singer, Maxwell, to serenade his bride as his wedding surprise to her.

For Woodrow, all he had to do was watch the clock and not miss a beat. He was not going to be the one to mess things up on this day—or any other. Woodrow was really anal, with a keen eye for every detail. He'd watched too many people come, and mostly go, under Juice's temperamental, no-tolerance-for-human-or-any-other-sort-of-error style of dealing with people. Woodrow had witnessed an assistant, who had booked Juice into the wrong Miami hotel, not just cussed out, but not able to find another job in the record industry after that.

Woodrow glanced at his watch again. It was time.

"Yo, young blood, get your car ready," he commanded the other driver. "You're the second in the procession to Tavern on the Green, behind me. I'm about to pull up to the front of the church. I'll check you when we get there. Cool?"

"Yeah, man," the other driver responded. "I'll check you there."

As Woodrow got into the car and started the ignition, there was a commotion inside the church.

Bang! Bang! Bang! Three shots rang out.

The doors of the church flew open.

Out of the church spilled a frantic herd of Guccis and Jimmy Choos, Brooks Brothers suits and Valentino gowns. Rich folks, far from concerned about appearances at this point, did their best impression of Marion Jones as they ran for their lives.

"They're shooting! They're shooting!" someone screamed.

"They killed Juice!"

"Juice is dead!"

SEVERAL YEARS EARLIER
New York City

Living on Central Park North, Carl and Linda had a spectacular view of Manhattan's celebrated playground. They inhabited the kind of sprawling apartment featured in the Sunday real estate section of the *New York Times*. A few years back they'd bought the apartment next door and broken down the walls to enlarge their original digs. The construction was part of the deal Carl had made with Linda. In order to make her happy about living in Harlem, Carl had promised he would have the remodeling done to her specifications. Raised in the slums of Detroit, Linda wanted a large home that didn't feel like an apartment.

Carl, on the other hand, enjoyed Harlem, not only because it was one of the fastest-growing markets in terms of real estate, but also because there was a lot of young money there in the hands of the inexperienced. He'd also been raised in Harlem and loved being surrounded by his people—in sharp contrast to his working life where he came across only a sprinkling of dark faces. He wanted his people to thrive, and he did what he could to share his knowledge to enable everyone around him to obtain wealth.

Carl had made his name on his instincts. As a major power broker on Wall Street, he'd quickly become an IPO whiz, someone everyone in his business respected. He knew when a company was about to go under, and he also knew when a company had the potential to make a comeback. He'd taken over three major companies and turned them into multimillion-dollar successes.

Carl Braxton was the funding source for many attempting to expand or start a major business. He was known as Mr. Money. His Harvard business and law degrees were his foundation, but his sharp instincts were what allowed him to rise. He went from Harvard to the mergers and acquisitions department of Bear Stearns, to his executive position at the country's largest bank, to starting his *own* investment bank.

But his ambitions were so much greater. Carl Braxton wanted a seat on the board of governors of the Federal Reserve, with the hope of becoming the first black chair.

The Federal Reserve was run by men with names like Mishkin, Kohn, Korzner, Greenspan, and Bernanke. Only five women had ever sat on the board of governors since its inception in 1914 and none of them had lasted the full fourteen-year term. Andrew Felton Brimmer had been the first black man to sit on the board and he hadn't served a full term either. Neither had Roger Ferguson, who'd been in a position to become the first black Federal Reserve chairman but had mysteriously resigned from his post as vice chair in 2006, eight years before his term would expire.

Not only was it improbable to get a seat on the board, which required an appointment by a sitting president, but to leapfrog over all those who had waited out five, eight, twelve years for a shot at the seat had to be impossible. But that's what drove Carl—the impossibilities. He loved that. The greater the odds against him, the more he was excited by the prospects.

He kept this latest desire close to the vest, not even his wife knew. Only Mortimer Zane, billionaire, longtime business associate, and the one man who could actually help Carl get there knew about his plan.

Tall and lean, wearing a long satin bathrobe, Linda gracefully strolled into the living room where Carl was standing, talking on his cell phone.

"Okay then," Carl said. "I'll see you next week. Looking forward to it."

He was speaking to Mortimer. But Carl was always careful to never utter a name aloud. He didn't know who might be listening.

Linda went into the kitchen. She noticed Carl's laptop on the counter and the latest *Wall Street Journal* scattered around. Carl frequently fell asleep reading the pages of various financial websites and watching stock prices. If he wanted to remain a part of the elite group of men who made millions if a stock gained a mere ten cents, or be in on the ground level of an IPO, he had to make the internet a part of his daily routine. Although he worked mostly from home, he made it his business to not let his work consume his home life.

Linda returned to the living room with a cup of coffee in each hand. She passed one to Carl, then sat quietly on the couch. Carl held up a finger, motioning to Linda that he'd be right back, as he stepped into another room.

She walked over to the window and out onto the balcony, imagining what her life might have been had she not gone to college and gotten her degrees. She could see a homeless man milling about Central Park, looking through the garbage. She turned her head and witnessed a dope addict copping drugs in a lightning-speed transaction from a man standing outside a bodega.

"Who was that?" Linda asked as Carl clicked off the phone and walked up behind her, wrapping his arm around her waist. She leaned back and rested her head on his strong shoulder.

"Oh, that was just business," he said. "I have an important meeting next week and I was getting some of the details."

He started to kiss Linda up and down her neck. Without letting go of her, Carl guided her back into the apartment. He threw his phone onto the couch as she began to shiver with desire. He undid the belt on her robe, searching for her silky skin.

"No, honey," Linda protested gently as she turned to face Carl, putting her arms around his waist. "I need to talk to you about something before we get into all of that."

"What is it?" he said, kissing her wistfully all over her face.

She took his hands in hers and led him to the couch.

"Honey, I gratefully appreciate everything you have done for Jacob. You treat him like he's your own son."

"I know, I know. Don't worry about it," said Carl, moving his hands up Linda's exposed thigh.

"Baby, really, this is serious," she said, closing her robe and moving his hands away.

Carl leaned back and sank into the couch.

"What's bothering you?" he asked, using the matter-of-fact tone that he usually reserved for business.

"Well," Linda said hesitantly, "Jacob wants to drop out of Princeton."

"What?" shouted Carl, instantly losing his hard-on as he rose to his feet, then placed his hands on his hips. "Doesn't that boy know the only way you can make it in this world nowadays is to have a college education? Doesn't he know what you went through to get an education so that he could have a better life?"

Carl was reacting the way Linda had expected. She had asked herself all the same questions over a week ago when Jacob had come to her with the announcement. She had recalled all the sacrifices she had made early on in her life for him. She thought about the day she'd learned she was pregnant by her high school sweetheart. She remembered the cold look in his eyes when he said it was not his and walked out the door. And she never forgot her mother's stinging words, which had motivated her to leave the house in which she had been raised. "Whatever comes out of your pussy, you're taking care of it, so you best start looking for a job now 'cause a diploma don't buy diapers." Linda didn't want to end up like the women in the building she grew up around—underachieving impoverished gossips.

Carl ignored the blank look on Linda's face.

"I mean, how does he plan on making a living? He can't live here if he's not in school. I won't tolerate someone hanging around not doing anything," Carl said, his voice rising.

"Babe, calm down," Linda said in a low voice. "I don't think anger will make him continue his studies. We have to do something that makes him see what a critical decision this is."

"Perhaps we have spoiled him," Carl interjected. "I thought giving him everything would motivate him to work hard. Maybe we just gave him too much and it has been too easy for him. If we put him out, he could see for himself what it takes to earn enough of a living to put a roof over his head and food on the table."

"No, I don't think that's the answer," Linda said. "I can't imagine him on the streets. He's not that kind of kid."

"Yeah, he's soft," Carl said, throwing his hands in the air.

"How can you say something like that? Before I met you, Jacob was always there in my defense, being the man of the house in his own way."

"You have to stop babying him," Carl said. "As a single mother you got two degrees, so I know that Jacob can finish his last year. I'm going to make him."

When Linda walked out of her mother's house forever, she'd had her high school diploma under her belt. She applied for every scholarship she could find. She settled on the University of Pittsburgh because it had a day-care program on campus that allowed her to go to school during the day. She found a small apartment nearby, which she shared with Audrey Powell, an ambitious schoolmate majoring in marketing. Audrey loved Jacob and volunteered to babysit while Linda worked at night.

After she graduated from the University of Pittsburgh, she moved to New York where she secured an internship on Wall Street. She lived in Brooklyn in the culturally rich Fort Greene area in a small studio with Jacob by her side. After she'd found a permanent position at Shearson Lehman, she met Carl. At the time, Carl was a big muckety-muck vice president and she a lowly account manager.

"Carl, I think if we handle this aggressively he'll probably go back to school, but his heart won't be in it," Linda said.

"I don't care about his heart," Carl said. "I care about his brain—and his future."

"Me, too, but I don't want to push him away. I want him to

be passionate about learning and not feel as if it's something we want for him. I want him to want it for *himself.*"

"I can't even believe that I was going to take him to the basketball game with me next week," Carl grumbled. "I have a bunch of skybox tickets from a business associate. I thought that would be a nice break from studying for Jacob. Now I see he wants his whole life to be one big break."

"Oh, no, let's still take him to the game," Linda said. "It might be good for him to be around our friends and see that it is unacceptable to drop out. Plus, you two have been getting along so well lately, I don't want anything to disrupt that."

"Don't even bring that up," Carl said, leaving the room.

Carl had been showering Linda's son with gifts since he'd come into Jacob's life. He'd wanted to make up for all the years Jacob didn't have a father and all the years he hadn't had one, too. Jacob was resistant at first, being protective of his mother. Linda, like many single mothers, had made her baby boy the center of her universe and Jacob had enjoyed the spotlight and was not interested in sharing his mother's love. The first few years of Linda and Carl's marriage were stressful because of Jacob's jealousy, but since he'd left for college, Jacob and Carl had gotten along well, especially after Carl bought him a car to use to travel back and forth to Princeton.

"Carl, I'll invite Audrey," Linda said. "We haven't seen her in a while and I'm sure Jacob will want to see his auntie Audrey. And maybe Audrey will meet one of your friends there and finally get herself a man."

Carl's laugh bellowed through the house. Linda enjoyed the sound of his deep laugh and began to think about how they'd met, the way he'd changed her life.

"Audrey ain't trying to find no man. That cold woman is married to her job," Carl said, laughing again.

"Don't let her exterior fool you. All women want a man, especially one who can take them away from their job!" Linda joked. "She just hasn't met the right one yet, like I have."

"Now ya talking, baby. Come on in here and let me love you up."

Linda stepped out of her robe, left it on the floor of the living room, and walked to the bedroom naked.

When Linda entered the workforce, the disciplined work ethic and determination she had exercised throughout her college years followed her. While she had good intuition, it was not enough to help her navigate the corporate work environment and office politics. For many years, she dutifully performed her work tasks, and when her boss needed her assistance for special projects, Linda was more than eager to help. In fact, those special projects assisted Linda in maintaining her enthusiasm for her position. Her job paid her decently, but she didn't feel her career was going anywhere, especially when younger white girls came in and Linda was repeatedly passed over for promotions that the others received. She was quick to blame her plight on racism. However, she would attend the promotion parties of her white coworkers and congratulate them with her usual friendly smile.

At one point in Linda's life, though, she'd become disenchanted by what was happening around her, seeing others move ahead of her at a fast pace, moving on to better salaries and bonus packages. Jacob was eight and had asked when he could have a room of his own. Linda knew it was time to leave her cozy studio apartment and find something bigger. She was also tired of the long commute from Brooklyn to Manhattan every day. The problem was, her salary did not allow her to afford a two-bedroom in the city and keep Jacob in the private school he attended.

While in the coffee room at work one day, Linda noticed an announcement for a department-head position. If she were to get the job, her salary would double. She was excited just thinking about it. That afternoon she scheduled an appointment with her boss.

What stood out about Linda's boss were her glasses. They were oversize dark ovals that made her eyes look as if you were staring into a magnifying glass. When Linda walked into Big Eyes's office, her boss didn't even look up from the piece of paper she was examining on her cherrywood desk.

"Have a seat," Big Eyes directed.

Linda sat in the seat opposite her boss. She did not say a word, thinking that her superior was engrossed in her paperwork. She looked around the sparsely decorated office. Across the room there was a red sofa and coffee table with two large comfortable-looking chairs. On the wall hung a huge Gustav Klimt print, rich with reds and golds. There were no file cabinets or bookshelves or clutter.

"And . . . ," Big Eyes said, still reviewing the spreadsheet.

Realizing her boss was waiting for her to say something, Linda turned her head back toward the desk, noticing for the first time a picture of Big Eyes smiling with feminist Gloria Steinem.

Linda began, "Well . . . I . . . just . . . want . . ."

"What? You want what?" Her boss put the document down, and when she did so her diamond ring hit her desk, sounding like a gavel.

Linda's palms were sweating.

"I want to be the next head of finance," Linda blurted out.

"Well, Linda, you have worked here for four years and—," started her boss.

"I know, I know, but there have been people who have worked here a shorter period of time and—," Linda stammered before she was interrupted.

"Linda, let me finish. You have worked here for four years and this is the first time you have asked for anything. I gave those other undeserving people promotions because they were constantly in my office asking for something."

Linda shifted in her seat, a little unsure about where her boss was going with this. Big Eyes's assistant discreetly walked into the room and removed the piece of paper on her boss's desk. She nodded her head and Big Eyes nodded back. The assistant then placed a new spreadsheet on the desk and left the room.

"I'm glad you have decided to grow with this company. When you don't ask for a promotion, higher-ups can only assume that you are content in your current position. I am glad you have finally put yourself in a position to use your obviously rich supply of talent," said her boss.

"Thank you very much!" Linda exclaimed.

"Wait a minute. Let me at least tell you that the job is yours first."

Big Eyes smiled and crossed her hands, sitting up straight, as if this were the first time she had laid eyes on Linda.

"Linda, the job is yours. You are the new head of finance."

Linda stood up, smiling, to shake her boss's hand. "When do I start?"

"Take the rest of the week to organize your desk. Take a week off, with pay, of course, then I'll see you on the twenty-seventh floor, where your new office will be. And congratulations!"

When Linda reached the door, she heard her boss say, "Part of being ready for a bigger life is having the guts to ask for it."

A week and a half later, in a brand-new outfit, Linda entered her office building with the enthusiasm she'd had on her first day with Shearson Lehman. She was ready for the challenges of her new position. When she stepped on the elevator, the congratulations began. When she walked into her new office, she was welcomed by two bouquets of flowers. She reached for the cards to see who they were from. The first one read, "Keep Asking," which was no doubt from her former boss. The second one read, "Congratulations! Looking forward to working with you. Carl."

Linda walked out of her office. A young white girl stood up.

"Yes, ma'am. I'm your assistant."

"Good morning. Do you know who Carl is?" Linda asked.

"He's the executive vice president of finance. You may know him as Mr. Braxton."

Linda realized she had read his name on many memos, but had never actually seen him. The company was large and had many employees and it was rare that everyone got to know one another. Company outings didn't help much either since most people mingled only with those on the same level.

"Here's your schedule for today. The first thing is a nine thirty meeting with all the financial heads. Here's the agenda for the meeting. It is in Conference Room B. Would you like coffee or anything?" said the eager young lady.

"No, I'm fine," Linda said, checking her watch. "I think I'll head down there now."

Everywhere Linda went, her coworkers acknowledged her accomplishment, including when she entered the conference room. A room full of graying men with bald spots seemed genuinely pleased by Linda's promotion. The few women in the room, all young and blond, did, too. A tray of bagels and muffins was set up in the corner. Linda walked over and put a piece of muffin on her plate. Just as she took a bite, Carl Braxton walked into the room.

"Hack! Hack! Hack!" At the sight of Carl, some of the bread had gone down the wrong way in Linda's throat.

One of the balding men got up to pat her on the back.

Carl ran to her side. "Linda, are you all right?"

Linda nodded her head, but still couldn't manage to speak. Carl gave her a cup of water, which cleared her throat. She smiled at everyone and sat down quietly, still unable to use her voice. She could not believe she had never laid eyes on this brother. He was stunning, brown skinned, with dark brown eyes and the whitest teeth she had ever seen. And his body! He was a few inches over six feet and was toned enough that the outline of his arm muscles was visible through his shirt. He was an incredibly handsome man.

Carl sat at the head of the table.

"Thanks to Linda, I don't have to open this meeting with one of my tired jokes. It seems everybody is up and ready to roll," Carl said, a smile on his face.

Linda joined the room in a slight laugh. She could not concentrate on Carl's words as he went over the company's first-quarter earnings for most of the meeting. She could only think about how long it had been since she'd found comfort in the arms of a man.

At the close of the meeting, Carl stopped Linda as she was on her way out.

"Be careful with the bagels they serve here. They are really dry," he joked.

"I'll keep that in mind," Linda said, finally finding her voice.

When she turned to leave, Carl gently held on to her arm.

"Over the years you have done a magnificent job on behalf of this company. I'm glad that we'll have more direct interaction."

"Thank you," Linda said shyly.

"Let's have dinner tonight so that I can bring you up to speed on everything at this level," Carl said in an inviting tone of voice.

"I don't usually . . . ," Linda started. "Of course. That sounds great!"

"I'll have my assistant give yours a call. I'll see you later this evening."

"That's a plan," Linda said, trying to sound with-it.

"I make it my business to know the new people who look like me," Carl said, almost whispering as he leaned in closer to Linda. "It can be tough sometimes. Look around. There aren't very many of us working here. So if you need anything or if anyone gives you a hard time, let me know."

By the time Linda walked back to her office, her assistant had the details about her nine o'clock dinner with Carl.

They met at Shelly's, a midtown restaurant known for its seafood. Carl walked in half a second after Linda.

"Welcome, Mr. Braxton, we haven't seen you in a while," exclaimed the maître d'. "Let me show you to your table. We love having you dine in our establishment."

The maître d' glided past the other tables and situated Carl and Linda in a large booth in the middle of the room, in clear view of the bar of iced seafood.

"Should I bring you your usual drink?" the maître d' asked.

"Yes, and the lady will have a dry vodka martini," Carl said matter-of-factly.

Linda thought of protesting, but she was excited by a man

who took control. She was used to ordering for her son; it was nice to have someone do it for her for a change.

"You don't usually do what?" Carl asked.

Linda gazed at him, perplexed.

"Earlier, when I asked you to dinner . . ."

"Oh, yes. Well, I was going to say that I didn't usually go out after work. I have a son and I like to be there for him at night," Linda confessed.

Carl hesitated for a moment, scratching his temple.

"Just let me know if I'm being too personal. Is there a father in the picture?"

"Unfortunately, Jacob doesn't know his father. He is a man I knew in Detroit, where I was raised," Linda announced reluctantly.

"I didn't mean to take you away from your son. Is he in good hands tonight?"

"Yes," Linda replied, feeling right away that Carl was concerned about her son's well-being. "He's with my friend Audrey, who was my college roommate. They have a long history."

They spent the entire evening talking about their personal lives, and not one word about business. The more they talked, the more Linda realized that this man was the answer to her prayers. They seemed to share the same dreams and aspirations.

When the company car pulled up in front of Linda's apartment, Carl got out to walk her to her door. He leaned in and gave her a kiss on the cheek.

"Carl, is this a date?" Linda asked after the welcome surprise.

"No, of course not. I don't date coworkers," Carl said with a smile.

Eventually, they began to meet on the weekends, and often

Carl would invite the apprehensive Jacob. A turning point was when Carl took them to the Hayden Planetarium. For the ten-year-old, seeing those stars and planets up close was thrilling. But it was more rewarding for Linda watching this man lovingly interact with her son. Carl guided Jacob from exhibit to exhibit, his hand resting gently on Jacob's shoulder. Jacob was wowed by every showcase, excited by the information Carl shared. When they came to the gigantic telescope, Carl lifted Jacob up so that he could reach the equipment. Carl told Jacob that each star represented a human life. And that when someone died on earth, a star went out in the sky. Jacob was enthralled.

Linda hadn't realized how necessary it was to have a man in her son's life. Jacob and Carl communicated differently. Maybe it was the strength of Carl's voice, but Jacob seemed to have a healthy respect for this man.

The night after the planetarium was the first time Carl and Linda made love. He was tender and passionate, revealing that his body thirsted for hers as much as hers did for his.

"If you're going to stay the night, you're telling me you're staying around for a while," Linda whispered in his ear.

Carl turned to say something in Linda's ear but instead grabbed her earlobe with his thick lips, licking around the outer rim and then jabbing his tongue softly into her ear. Linda had never felt that sensation before as the heat grew between her legs.

"I'm not going anywhere," said Carl.

The next morning Carl got up and cooked breakfast for Linda and Jacob.

"Jacob, I would like to marry your mother," Carl announced. Linda and Jacob both sat there with their mouths hanging open. "Do I have your permission?"

They were a family from that moment on.

Chapter

4

"S ir," Carl's assistant said, attempting to get the VP's attention.

"What can I do for you?"

"This package arrived and I think you should open it."

"What do you mean? You open all my mail," said Carl, mystified.

"Well, it arrived in a large black box with a gold ribbon. I opened the box, only to find a smaller box. In gold letters it said 'Personal and Confidential.' I opened that box and there was another smaller box. It had gold letters with the same message as the previous one, only this time the letters were larger."

Carl took the box from her. It was light in weight. He shook it and it didn't make a sound. He sniffed it and it smelled faintly of wood, like all good paper stock. He pushed it to one corner of his desk and went back to reading the document before him. A short while later, his curiosity got the better of him and he picked up the box again.

Maybe it's a special gift from Linda.

It was about the size of a Tiffany tennis bracelet box. Carl turned it around and over and over in his hands before finally opening it. The box was empty. Annoyed, Carl threw it in the wastebasket underneath his desk. When he did so, the lid of the box landed face up. There was a date, time, and place scrolled in gold and a gold key taped to the top of the lid. There was no signature.

What the hell?

Carl placed the lid of the box in his briefcase to take home with him. He rested his elbows on his desk and began to rub his chin. Unable to concentrate, he decided to go home early.

A similar mysterious box arrived on the desks of six other men that day, including Xavier Prince, whose assistant just placed it on his desk, next to his briefcase.

"Fuck you, racist motherfuckers!" shouted Xavier into the receiver after the party on the other end had long since hung up.

He stood up, forcing his chair into the wall unit behind him, causing all the trophies and statues to rock and the glass to vibrate.

Xavier Prince had won every award and title one could hope for. Overseas, he was a Michael Jordan to the Italians. He had brought home eight consecutive league titles, led the league in scoring for eight of the thirteen years he'd played for Il Madoro. His likeness was associated with everything from Fila sneakers to Cioko Rice, the Italian Cocoa Puffs.

Xavier Prince, once the most heralded player to come out of the Bronx, was fated to be the next NBA superstar. A torn ACL in his junior year of college and a slow recovery made his stock drop. Instead of taking the second-round selection with the Toronto Raptors, he'd decided to take his chances with an offer from Il Madoro. His agent said it was one of the most lucrative deals in Italian-league history.

"Wouldn't you rather be a ready-made star in Italy than have to prove yourself with a bad team in the NBA?" his agent said, selling him on it.

It didn't take much selling. Xavier was bitter about the fact that teams who'd said they were going to take him in the top-ten picks of the NBA draft didn't take him at all. He felt lied to and betrayed. But more important, Xavier felt that he wanted to make them pay, and promised himself he would one day own an NBA team.

The best revenge, his mother always told him, was success. Xavier decided he would go to Italy and make every NBA team wish they had taken him.

His agent did not lie. Xavier Prince became an instant star. His chocolate brown good looks and boyish smile made the women swoon. His ability to perform almost Cirque du Soleil acrobatics on the court made men drool. The calls from the NBA started coming after Xavier was named rookie of the year in the Italian league, leading his team to its first title in nine years. He didn't just take a losing team to the championship, he made the owners of the team even richer, as the arena was sold out for every home game and Xavier Prince jerseys became the hottest-selling item—even outselling Italian soccer star Marco Materazzi.

His agent called him one afternoon, practically hyperventilating.

"Xavier, are you sitting down?"

"Yeah, man, what's up?" he said.

"I just got off the phone with the Miami Heat," the agent said. "They want to offer you a three-year deal worth more than nine million dollars! You've arrived! You have made it to the NBA!"

Xavier was silent.

"Hello? Xavier, did you hear me?" the agent said. "You can

have a contract to play in the NBA. I told you it would all work out!"

"I'll get back to you," Xavier said, hanging up the phone.

Being abroad had changed Xavier, changed his dreams. Living in America as a young black man, he'd wanted fame and money more than anything. But living among the passionate Italians, he was learning that life was about something deeper.

When he was not in the gym or on the court, he spent a great deal of time observing Italian people. As in most European countries, the majority of the people were not rich-rich. But they seemed to have enough to make them smile and greet strangers and friends with the same elated *"Buongiorno!"* They kissed and hugged openly in public piazzas. They groped each other lustfully in small dark restaurants. In the market, the women wore sling-back stilettos and low-cut dresses, unafraid of their sexuality, showing affection to women and men with equal passion. The businessmen worked hard, but they took three-hour lunch breaks, leaving enough time to eat and make love before returning to their jobs. Then, at the end of the workday, they would arrive home for a lavish long dinner with their family and, after that, more lovemaking.

Observing Italian culture, and getting to know the people, had given Xavier invaluable insight. He knew that money couldn't buy you good friends, happiness, a sense of self-acceptance, or intelligence. The country was entirely different from America, and he was not ready to return to his cold, money-grubbing homeland. He had fallen in love with Italy.

Xavier decided to share the news of his NBA offer with the owner of his Italian team. Marcello Mastrelli did not congratulate Xavier, instead he invited him to his villa in Tuscany for a week. The owner of Il Madoro had a stunning palatial home, marble floors and pillars throughout. Xavier was offered his own wing for his stay. The view from his bedroom window was breathtaking. He could see the tops of trees that seemed to roll on for miles, covering layered hills. Xavier was free to roam around the property and explore the city at his leisure. His only obligation was to meet Marcello and his family every day for a slow, delicious meal.

Marcello's wife was a gorgeous, small-waisted woman with large breasts. However, the feature about her that captivated Xavier was her long eyelashes and her dark eyes, which sparkled every time she looked at Marcello. The owner's three daughters and son exhibited the same light-filled eyes of admiration when they looked at their father.

On Xavier's final night in Tuscany, Marcello asked him to have a drink in his study. Xavier had abandoned his casual clothing for the evening and chosen to put on a suit. He was glad he had when he discovered that Marcello had done the same. Instinctively, he knew it was time to get down to business and that the vacation was over.

Marcello had made Xavier the highest-paid player in the Italian league—a gamble considering Xavier's college injury.

"Have you decided what you want to do about the NBA offer?" Marcello said in his Italian-accented English as he poured Xavier's drink into a crystal glass.

"I'm not interested in returning to the States yet," replied Xavier.

"Very well," said Marcello, lighting and taking a puff of his cigar. "I will give you more money—not as much as your NBA offer. But I've decided to give you something more important. I will teach you how to control your destiny. I will give you the key to happiness."

During the following couple of years, Marcello enriched

Xavier's life by sharing his business and investment smarts. All the while, he emphasized to Xavier that money did not equal power.

"Real power is the ability to *refuse* money," Marcello told Xavier one day.

He informed him that a man must be clear and honest about what gives him pleasure.

"A man should be trustworthy and have a strong sense of integrity," was Marcello's mantra. "A man's material desires should not outweigh what he is willing to work for." Marcello explained that many people will say they want this or that, but the key is their willingness to work for it. It was a message that should have come from Xavier's father. And while he had many male mentors, most of them coaches, none had the impact of Marcello. It was Marcello who truly helped Xavier understand what it meant to be a man.

Xavier had arrived in Italy a scared, insecure athlete. He eventually departed for the States a fearless man. He was no longer obsessed with luxury items and what other people thought of him. He abandoned his desire to be famous, and replaced it with a commitment to emotional self-satisfaction. He wanted to make sure that he lived life, experienced it, and did not become simply an onlooker who envied the lives and possessions of others. He would make every day an adventure, a challenge. With his newfound wisdom, Xavier left Italy with a bank account in the stratosphere. The property that Marcello had told him to buy in Florence, Siena, and Pisa had tripled in value. But the money was nothing compared with the invaluable insight he had gained from Marcello.

You lousy motherfuckers!" Xavier yelled into the phone again.

He paced around his spacious New York office looking like George Jefferson throwing someone out of his home for disrespecting him. The only difference was that no one else was in the room with him. And there was no one on the other end of the phone.

He had said good-bye a full two minutes before. But his anger was still bubbling over.

"It's never enough for you, is it!" Xavier spit out to himself through clenched teeth. "It's never enough!"

Xavier had gathered the majority portion of the $230 million required to buy the basketball team. He had followed the proper procedures. He did everything he was told he had to do—he raised the money, he put in his bid. But it still wasn't enough. They told him that he couldn't have majority ownership. The league had the right to decline any offer, and they didn't have to have a good reason. At least they were "allowing" Xavier a figurehead position for the millions he was willing to pay. They told him that he could be the face of the Atlanta Hawks, he could make the appearances as the "owner"—he would look like the owner—but he would still be only a minority owner, with no real power and no real share of the profits.

"Of course, you will be well compensated, Xavier," said the NBA commissioner. "You will have all the benefits of being an owner without the headaches. I think it's a great deal for you."

How condescending. Calling me Xavier like we're friends. I'm Mr. Prince! Who the fuck does he think he's dealing with? Some dumb nigger? I've done my homework. I know what the deal is!

But Xavier only said: "Thank you, Commissioner. It's a great deal. I will consult my advisers about it and get back to you."

Xavier had learned diplomacy from Marcello—that, and to never use his own money. Xavier had saved practically every dime from his playing days, which was easy since the team paid for lodging and meals and Xavier never needed a flashy car, jewelry, or any other big-ticket items to make him feel like a man. He was the poster boy for living below his means and now he was in a position to realize his dream—owning an NBA franchise.

It was something Xavier had told himself he would do on the draft day when he'd slipped into the second round. He'd told himself that if they didn't want him, he would come back and own a team. They would have to contend with him when it counted.

Anyone can be a trained monkey, he thought, running up and down a court in shorts. They will give a man millions for that. Whites always pay to be entertained, especially when it meant they were paid more than the entertainer. True respect is found in the boardrooms and in the back rooms and in the golf clubs. If you can make them respect you there, or at least deal with you as a man, then you have arrived.

Xavier was close, so close to arriving.

He was going to hold on to his temper and come up with a new Plan A. Xavier knew he was being shafted. He believed he was more than qualified to run a team. But it just seemed impossible to break into the old boys' club; it was starting to feel personal.

This was important to him, it wasn't just about vindication. Xavier knew that ownership, real ownership, would have an impact on the way he—and perhaps black men in general—would be perceived. He was a king in Italy. But in America he was just another black man. Owning a team was about taking power from the majority's hands and putting it in his own. There was no way he would take a *minority* ownership position. There was no way he was going to accept a lesser place than he deserved.

To relieve his tension, Xavier decided to leave early for the day and go shoot some hoops at the West Fourth Street cage in the Village. This particular court provided the most challenging games for an old pro. And the games always brought out a crowd.

When Xavier was on the court, he was just a dude playing basketball, not a multimillionaire businessman. He could lace up his sneakers and begin shooting around, feeling the rush of adrenaline come back to him. He could bump, shoot, run, get knocked down, and get back up and all his troubles could just fade away. He was the man in this arena. He owned the ball.

Xavier couldn't wait to get to the court. He changed his clothes and grabbed his bag. Before he left, he remembered the black gift box and opened it. His laughter grew louder and louder as he opened each box within each box. When he finally got to the smallest and saw the writing inside the lid, he laughed the loudest.

"Okay, you have my attention," he said to the box, still chuckling.

He threw the invitation into his bag and headed to the courts. He also double-checked his briefcase to make sure he had tonight's skybox ticket to the Knicks game.

Audrey leaned into her bathroom mirror, checking for dark circles under her eyes. At forty-one she felt that her days of being drop-dead gorgeous were numbered. But on this day she still had it all—flawless, wrinkle-free skin and healthy strong hair. Aside from her looks, she also had an outstanding career and a beautiful home. She applied her makeup and let down her hair. Audrey believed it was her hairdresser who gave her the look and the confidence to carry out the attitude she knew was required to get ahead and stay ahead. She knew it was her looks that had gotten her promoted quickly through the corporate, shit-layered cake.

She knew plenty of men and women of all races who were smarter and more talented. Audrey had passed them on her way up the corporate ladder, for no reason other than her looks and how she carried herself. It was something her mother had drilled into her head at a very young age.

"Baby, it's not what you say, it's how you say it," Audrey's mother would preach. "I know you heard that one before. But remember, if you look good enough, all they'll remember is that you look good."

Audrey was smart, and she was competent at her job, but she knew also that it was never about *what* she knew, it was more about how she looked and who liked her. She had a knack for ingratiating herself with higher-ups. She didn't consider it brownnosing; it was business. Maintaining friendships with the men in charge kept her in the loop and on the promotion list. She would walk right up to the line with these men, giving them a whiff. But she knew that crossing that line could cause her more trouble than it was worth. It was better to have men wanting her, hoping that they might one day get her—while she knew all the while that would never happen—than to give in to their desires. The most desirable woman, she discovered, was one men wanted but never had. It was the mystery that kept them coming.

So Audrey worked on her golf and tennis games. She learned to hold her liquor and could drink most under the table. She even smoked cigars and would frequent the cigar bars where big business went down.

She also spent a lot of time in the gym, perfecting her body. She was tighter and more toned than the youngest administrative assistant. Audrey had the arms of Angela Bassett in *How Stella Got Her Groove Back*, and a butt that a quarter could do a backflip off.

This attention to those details was all about control for Audrey. She believed that she could control every aspect of her life and, as a result, have every single thing she wanted. Her life was ruled by regimen. Audrey arrived at her office at 7:45 A.M. every morning, fifteen minutes ahead of schedule. She wanted to be the first one in and the last to leave.

Twenty-two years and a management position at her company brought her the luxury of a four-and-a-half-day workweek. After work, Audrey headed to the gym, except on Wednesdays and Fridays. Wednesday was food-shopping day—organic and all natural. Every Friday she left the office at noon exactly. On Fridays Audrey went shopping for everything from clothes to makeup. Every Saturday she had her standing hair appointment with Eriberto.

Audrey took the elevator down to the garage and got in her car. She pulled out of the parking space and drove to the exit, where she was waiting for the electric arm to go up when she heard her cell ringing. She saw Linda's name pop up on the screen and she hit Accept.

"Hey, Linda, what's going on?" said Audrey.

"Well, nothing really," she said. "I was just wondering if you could go with me, Carl, and Jacob to a basketball game."

"This had better not be one of your fix-ups. I swear, Linda! I'm still not over that last one you and Carl thought would be perfect for me."

All of Audrey's hookups started and ended in the same way—a whole cycle of going places she didn't really want to go, having company she didn't really want to have and having to consider that person's feelings, ultimately ending in having to screen her phone calls because she didn't want to be bothered anymore.

"I know you're laughing," Audrey continued.

"Look, I'm not laughing," Linda said, trying to stifle chuckles. "Okay, okay. I *am* laughing. But it's not like that this time. I'm really not trying to hook you up."

"So what is it this time?" said Audrey, rolling her eyes as she turned onto the Garden State Parkway.

"It's just a basketball game," Linda said. "We have a fully catered skybox at Madison Square Garden. And afterward we're having drinks at Del Frisco's."

Linda closed her eyes and crossed her fingers.

"Okay, I'll go," Audrey said, relenting. "But I swear, you got one person to introduce me to and it's off! I just want to laugh and have a good time with you and Carl and Jacob."

"Great! A car will be picking me up and making its way to you shortly after, but I'll give you a call when I'm on my way," said Linda. "Carl and Jacob will already be in New York, so you and I will have the whole ride for some girl talk."

"Okay, talk to you later," said Audrey, smiling.

Audrey decided not to run her usual errands and instead went shopping for a killer outfit. While she gave Linda a hard time about hooking her up with someone, Audrey still wanted to make sure she was the center of attention: *Look but don't touch!*

Shopping was one of Audrey's favorite things to do, second only to *wearing* the killer outfit and watching all the male eyes in the room leave their wives and follow her across the room as she watched their wives pretend not to see who it was their husbands could not stop looking at.

Dressing for the game, Audrey decided it was going to be a diamond night. She selected her yellow diamond studs and a yellow diamond bracelet. She put on her custom-fitted jeans, the halter top she'd found at Max Mara, and the six-inch Gucci sandals she'd bought at the Garden State Mall. It was a simple outfit, but stunning enough for the occasion.

Linda arrived at seven fifteen sharp to pick Audrey up for their ride into New York from Bergen County, New Jersey. It would be less than a thirty-minute drive across the George Washington Bridge and down the West Side Highway.

"Hey, girl!" said Linda, admiring her friend's shoes as she got into the limo.

"Hi, sweetie," responded Audrey, giving her a hug. "You look awesome!"

Linda sported a sexy new haircut, a sassy bob. They started their ride in silence, which was unusual, but Linda didn't want to rush right in and begin talking about Jacob wanting to leave school. She wanted to be a girlfriend for a moment before turning into a wife and mother, roles that had become her whole life after Carl had convinced her years ago to leave her job.

"So, girl, how is that handsome man of yours?" Audrey said, finally breaking the silence.

"Thank God, he is still Mr. Wonderful. I don't know what I would do without him," Linda said, staring out the window and smiling. "He's the one who encouraged me to get this haircut. Everybody says I look like Halle Berry now."

The ladies laughed uproariously.

"I bet he did. He's always fussing over you. He probably picked out your outfit, too," Audrey teased.

"Well . . ."

The two women laughed again.

"He wants you to look just right next to him. The perfect couple attending black-tie affairs and entertaining in your home," Audrey said cattily.

"Girl, stop. I'm beginning to think you're jealous," Linda said, lightly punching Audrey in the arm.

"I don't know. Maybe a little bit," confessed Audrey. "Do you really like not working?"

"I do. Probably too much. There's nothing like being able to just think about making your family happy and having the resources to do so."

"You don't get bored or feel not stimulated intellectually?" Audrey asked.

"Not at all. It gives me great pleasure to take care of my home and the men in my life. Plus, I go to museums, art galleries, and sightsee in New York. I also read a lot. I read the *Times* every day to ensure that I know what's going on in the world. It helps me come up with substantial conversations at the many functions Carl and I attend—which feels like a job sometimes. I also read a lot of books. You know I like nonfiction about spirituality, health, and home decorating. And I hate to admit it, but I love those trashy street novels, for a break."

"I can't think of the last time I actually read a whole book or even had the time to think about who I am," complained Audrey.

"I never thought I would be this happy not working, but I enjoy propelling my man forward," Linda said. "And it's Carl's goal to one day not work himself. He told me the other day that there was just one more deal he wanted to make that would set us up for the rest of our lives. It has something to do with financing the gentrification of Harlem so that black people won't be pushed out. Once that's done, he'll be able to spend his days with me. He even suggested that perhaps we spend a year in Africa."

"You sound like a 1950s housewife," admonished Audrey.

"And, girl, what is wrong with that?" Linda shot back, slightly annoyed. "Black women have been working too hard and for too long trying to support and hold on to our men. Men who, in too many cases, gave up on themselves a long time ago."

"Lately I've been feeling that I'm ready for a real relationship, maybe even marriage," Audrey confided.

"What is it you got bottled up in that big head of yours?" asked Linda, fixing Audrey's hair around her shoulders as if she were her child.

"Damn, I think it's so freaking scary when you do that," said Audrey, waving a hand at Linda.

"Do what?" asked Linda.

"That motherly thing. I swear it makes you damn near a superpower," replied Audrey, laughing. "I don't know what it is, really. I think I'm lonely, or bored, or incomplete, or something else. I've been telling everyone for so long how happy I am with my single womanhood that I don't want to prove them right."

"Oh, so you do need me to fix you up after all?" Linda said, making Audrey laugh.

"Come on now!"

"Okay. You *were* happy," Linda said. "I could tell you were happy. But if you're not happy now, there is no shame in change. You shouldn't live your life trying to prove or disprove anything to anyone, Audrey."

"Then the other thing is, I'm forty-one years old and it feels like I've waited too long to feel this way and be able to do anything about it," Audrey lamented, leaning her head back against the headrest and trying to avoid choking up.

"I think you know it's never too late, baby, and you're too beautiful not to find someone who was born just for you," consoled Linda, empathizing with all of her friend's emotions. "Look, tonight we are going to laugh our asses off at Carl trying to be all schmoozy, and we will get to drink all we want 'cause we don't have to drive."

"How's my *real* man doing?" Audrey inquired with a giggle.

"Jacob has lost his damn mind, girl. He's talking about dropping out of school." Linda paused long enough to roll her eyes before getting out of the car, which had pulled up in front of Madison Square Garden.

The crowd at the Garden was its usual—loud and rowdy.
Whether the Knicks were on a championship run or at the
bottom of the Eastern Conference, the Garden crowd showed
unbridled support—or straight-up, in-your-face disdain. They
were extreme in either direction. During the period in 2007
when then-coach Isiah Thomas was making a mess with his off-
court antics, and the team was performing abysmally on the
court, the Garden was selling out. Fans showed up in droves just
to boo and chant, "Isiah must go!" Only in New York could just
as many fans show up when the team was losing.

Linda and Audrey bypassed the rowdy crowds of people—
some of whom had started drinking way before coming to the
Garden—after picking up their tickets. They headed for the VIP
elevator, reserved for family members of players and other spe-

cial people. The skyboxes hovered over the cheap seats, with a perfect bird's-eye view of center court. They were complete with forty-two-inch plasma TVs, for those who wanted to get the game and the commentary from the MSG broadcasters, and a full, open bar with gourmet food.

"What kept you guys? Never mind. I'm sure you're to blame for the tardiness, Audrey," teased Carl, winking at Audrey.

Audrey playfully rolled her eyes at Carl and waved him off.

The skybox was nearly full. As at any sports event, there were more men than women. And handsome men at that, Audrey noticed. They all looked sophisticated and well-to-do, except for a few thuggish ones a couple of boxes over.

Among the sea of handsome men was her little Jacob, who was growing into a fine man, as was his roommate, LaJuan. Audrey hadn't seen LaJuan in some time. He had changed so much. Before, he had worn the kind of bummy, eccentric clothing of a college student. Now he was sporting a more mature look, a black cashmere sweater and black-and-silk wool trousers, accessorized with a white-gold chain and a Rolex.

"I'm so glad you ladies made it here safe and sound," said Carl, breaking Audrey out of her reverie. "You both look beautiful. Let me introduce you to everyone."

Carl escorted his wife and Audrey around the room with skill and ease, making small talk with nearly every other person in the room, about ten men and four women in addition to Audrey and Linda. In comparison with Audrey and Linda, the other women looked as if they had on too much makeup, but not enough clothing, and they were much younger. As they approached two women deep in conversation, Audrey overheard one of them say, "Girl, I was telling the brotha he didn't have enough money to get with me when his phone ran out of minutes."

When Carl introduced them, these women offered big, breathy hellos, but seemed at a loss for additional conversation. Their smiles never deflated, though.

Audrey was struck by a man Carl didn't introduce to her. He was standing unassumingly to the side and their eyes locked. She was distracted, as Carl was introducing her to some person whose name she wouldn't remember and whose face was just a blur.

She broke away after just long enough and headed for the man in the corner, which wasn't Audrey's style. She usually waited for men to come to her.

"Hi," she said, not having a game plan and being completely out of her element.

"Hi," the mysterious man said back.

"I'm Audrey," she said, putting out her hand. *Am I supposed to put out my hand to shake? Is this appropriate?*

"I'm Bones," he said, taking her hand, not shaking it, just holding it gently. Audrey felt a sensation that made her want to snatch her hand away, as if she'd been shocked by a bolt of electricity. He eventually let her hand go and with that she was able to breathe again.

"Bones?" asked Audrey. "That's an unusual name."

"It's a childhood nickname that kind of stuck," he said.

"I won't ask," she said. "But I'm sure there's a story there."

"Yeah," he said nervously. "It's pretty boring, though."

"I doubt that!" she said.

Before they could get into a deeper conversation, Linda came rushing over and grabbed Audrey by the arm, oblivious to Audrey's connection with this man who, despite his size, she barely noticed.

"Girl, come say hello to Jacob!" she said, pulling Audrey away.

Audrey glanced back at Bones with an apologetic smile. And he gave her a nod, letting her know it was okay.

This box was crowded and the two waded through the sea of "important" people to Jacob and his friend. Linda was pulled away to do more schmoozing with and for Carl.

"Aunt A!" Jacob said, jumping up.

"Hey, baby! I'm so glad to see you," she said, giving Jacob a hug and a kiss and taking a seat. "Look at you! Getting more and more handsome by the day!"

"You lookin' outta this world yourself," he said, rubbing his chin. "If you hadn't changed my diapers as a kid, I would be tryin' to make a move."

Audrey playfully struck Jacob against the side of the head.

"Puu-lease, I'm not even trying to date no college dropout," she said. "How would I look picking my man up from the late shift at McDonald's?"

"That's cold, Aunt A," Jacob said, deflated. "It figures Mom would have told you. I'm just ready to make my own money. Maybe Mom is okay with depending on someone else, but that ain't my thing."

"Last time I checked, you haven't wanted for a thing," she reminded him. "In fact, if you ask me, you've gotten enough shit for three kids. All your parents want is for you to graduate from college and you're not grateful enough to do that?"

"Oh, Aunt A, it ain't even like that." Jacob was getting defensive. "LaJuan is making moves and I just want to get mine."

Jacob was nervous, running his hands over his clean-shaven head.

"LaJuan is still in school, right?"

"Yeah, for now," Jacob lied. "But next semester we're both dropping out. We have a plan. We're going into business together."

"And that can't wait another year or two until after you graduate? Boy, get out of my face. Negro foolishness makes my stomach turn."

Fed up, Audrey waved her hand as a signal that Jacob was dismissed.

"You are hard on a brother," Jacob said solemnly.

Audrey gently grabbed Jacob's hand. "No, honey, life is hard. I just want the best for you," she said, leaning in closer. "You're probably just restless. That kind of energy gets you in trouble. Finish school!"

Audrey needed to stretch her legs. She got up and went to the open bar to get a drink. While standing there, she saw a seat at the front of the room with a clear view of the game. Audrey was a basketball fanatic—she even loved college basketball—and the Los Angeles Lakers were in town. Basketball took her back to her college days, when she was a fixture at every single game. She'd known every player and had even dated a few.

Audrey walked to her seat overlooking the huge, stage-like court. She glanced down to see if she recognized any of the celebrities in the front row. While the skyboxes were nice, there was nothing like sitting courtside, on the floor. From those seats you could feel every gallop by the massive players and practically smell their sweat.

As Audrey settled in to watch the game, the team also began to settle down and execute, causing the crowd to erupt. When the home team's star power forward went baseline for a slam dunk to tie the score, it brought everyone in the arena to their feet.

"Those damn Knicks always play well against good teams," Audrey muttered under her breath, although she couldn't help but cheer. She, like most tristaters, had a love-hate thing going with the Knicks.

A figure walked into the room and sat a few seats from her. He was a tall man Audrey thought she recognized. Before she'd figured out where she knew him from, she was distracted by the crowd below and a few in the room who were actually there to see the game.

"The Knicks just went ahead!" screamed a guy who was standing at the skybox glass, excited. "That's what I'm talkin' 'bout!"

She looked to her right and spotted Bones. He had moved closer to the glass to see the game. One of the pretty young things from earlier glided over to sit next to him. Audrey tried to ignore the two as she stood up to take in the final quarter of the game. She couldn't help but be intrigued by Bones, who seemed more into the game than into the woman now sitting next to him. The woman kept trying to talk to him, while his eyes were fixed on the court. Finally, Bones whispered something to her and she walked away shaking her head and rolling her eyes. Bones's demeanor never changed. Audrey saw all of that, while still completely into the game.

Quietly, the man she thought she recognized, who was sitting to her left, was into the game, too, so much so that he never looked in Audrey's direction.

Now, how could he sit there and not even notice all of this?

She glanced over at him and then went back to watching the game. Then she paused, checking him out again. She knew the face, but she couldn't remember from where. The couple of glasses of wine she'd had didn't help jog her memory. The man turned and caught the gorgeous Audrey staring.

"What? Do I have something on my shirt?" asked Xavier, pretending to check his shirt for stains.

"I know you," Audrey responded. "But I just can't put my finger on it."

Xavier smiled.

"I've got it!" Audrey exclaimed. "You went to Pittsburgh. You were on the basketball team. I went to every single game!"

"Yes, I did," said Xavier. "Glad to hear you attended my games. My name is Xavier Prince. And you are . . . ?"

"Audrey . . . Audrey Williams," she replied. "Would you believe that this is the first live game I've been to in a while? And what about you? Are you involved in basketball still?"

"Um, I guess you could say that," he said. "What are you into?"

"I'm a vice president at Stark-optics," said Audrey, amazed by how his face—and his physique—hadn't changed in over twenty years.

Just as he was about to speak, Xavier's phone rang. Reluctantly, he excused himself and took the call, walking out of the skybox with the phone to his ear.

Audrey turned her attention back to the game. There was less than three minutes left and the Knicks had lost their lead and were down by five.

Xavier came back, still holding the phone to his ear. He held out his card, then placed it in Audrey's hand. Audrey tried hard to hide the girlishly shy behavior he was provoking in her.

This has got to stop!

"Please call me and then I'll have your number," said Xavier, putting his hand over the receiver. "I have to take this call, but I would really love to hear from you."

Xavier went back to his call, "Yes, I have the . . ." Xavier headed for the door, but turned and waved good-bye to Audrey before leaving the skybox.

The Knicks were still losing, but they were making it a game in the final minute and a half, pulling to within two on a three-pointer by their star guard. Audrey took her eyes away from the game to punch Xavier's digits into her cell.

"Who was that?" Linda had sneaked up behind her and now took a seat.

"Would you believe that he went to Pitt with us?" Audrey said. "He was one of the stars of the basketball team until he got hurt. Last I remember, he went to play in Italy. It's a shame I didn't get to know him in school."

Audrey looked at the number on the card and checked it again with what she'd entered in her phone to make sure it was right.

"He's very handsome!" said Linda. "Girl, Carl really had me putting on the charm with these people of his tonight. I'm sick of my own phony ass! I'm about to go to the ladies' room. Please get me a fresh drink. I'll be right back."

Audrey used the time alone to sneak a few glances at Bones. He must have been a mind reader, as he got up from his seat and confidently sat in the seat next to hers.

"I've got to say that I think you are outstanding," he announced in his smooth baritone voice.

"Excuse me?" said Audrey, surprised and not knowing exactly what to say after such a direct statement.

"I've been watching you all night," he said. "I know that sounds corny, like some line, but it's true."

Feeling vulnerable with Bones in control of the conversation, Audrey flipped the script.

"I've been watching you, too," she said. "So what was it you said to that woman?"

"I don't like nosy women," said Bones matter-of-factly.

Audrey's mouth hung open. Bones leaned in so that he was a breath away from her face.

"But I do like you," he said. "So don't be scared of a real man."

Audrey could feel herself becoming aroused. Not knowing what to do or say, she turned her head and stared at the players running up and down the court, not truly taking in what was happening or who had the ball as the seconds wound down. The Knicks were going to lose this game.

"A lot of people want what they want," he said, attempting to answer Audrey's question. "But they can't always have what they want if it's not what you want."

"Well, what do you want?" Audrey looked at Bones, surprised and intrigued by his words.

"You," he said.

"Well, what if you're not what I want?" Audrey said, playing coy.

Bones just looked at her and smiled.

It was a smile that brought a sweetness to a face that had definitely seen hard times. It was a smile that melted Audrey from the inside and betrayed her from the outside because it forced her to smile, too. The two didn't have to say another word.

Linda returned just in time to break the thick silence that had formed between them. She hung over her friend's shoulder, a drink in one hand, and extended the other to Bones.

"I'm Linda, Audrey's best friend. And you are . . . ?" she asked.

"Linda, this is Bones," Audrey said, not letting him answer.

"Nice to meet you," Linda said. "Hey, Bones, we have reservations after the game at Del Frisco's. Would you like to join us?"

"I'd like that a lot," answered Bones, who was smiling without showing his teeth. "A lot."

The three of them sat intently watching the final few seconds of the game. Everyone rose to their feet as the guard threw up a three-pointer that would have tied the score and sent the game into overtime but bounced off the back of the rim and rolled out of bounds as the buzzer sounded.

Dinner at Del Frisco's after the game was cool, but it was too much small talk, Carl and Linda dominating the conversation, trying to play detective and find out as much as they could about Bones. A man not entertained by small talk, Bones patiently fielded their questions for Audrey's benefit.

"So, where did you grow up?" Carl fired off.

"Do you have any siblings?" Linda said, immediately after Carl.

"And what do you do for a living?" Carl asked before Bones could answer the previous question.

"Hold up, hold up!" begged Bones. "The first two questions don't even matter. When you get down to it, we're all from the same place. And all black people are my brothers and sisters."

Carl stuck his hand out to give Bones a pound. Bones left him hanging and continued, "I'm a landlord."

"A landlord!" Carl exclaimed. "So you own real estate, huh? That's good. Where? What do you bring in in a month?"

For most, that question would have seemed like overstepping the bounds, but Carl didn't believe there were bounds when it came to money. He was fascinated by money and those making it.

"You get paid, though, right?" Carl persisted.

Bones shoveled some food into his mouth as if he hadn't heard Carl.

"You enjoying your meal, baby?" Bones asked Audrey.

"Indeed."

They couldn't trip Bones up. He was too good. Audrey was impressed with the way he handled himself. Most—even the most accomplished—could be intimidated or were taken aback by Carl, who could be very aggressive with getting what he wanted. But Bones was at home in his own skin, Audrey thought.

She enjoyed his company so much that she took him up on his offer to drive her home.

"Audrey, we came together, we should leave together," Linda said, pulling her friend to the side. "What if he's some sort of mass murderer or rapist or something? Remember Robert Chambers, the preppy killer? He was all cute and sexy, too."

"Girl, you need to stop!" Audrey responded in a low voice. "You know he's not a killer. I'm going to let this man drive me home so I can get to know him better."

"Okay. But you better not let him fuck you!" Linda demanded.

"Yes, Mother, no fucking on the first date," Audrey said sarcastically. "I got it."

Linda sucked her teeth, grabbed her friend, and gave her a huge bear hug.

"You take care and call me when you get in, no matter what time," Linda pleaded. "And keep your phone close to you in case you have to dial 911."

Audrey rolled her eyes.

The ride home with Bones was quiet. Audrey didn't know what to say. She didn't want to ask him any questions after what Carl and Linda had put him through over dinner. She let the silence hang in the air and pretended to take in the scenery. Bones kept his eyes on the road.

"So, do you have a girlfriend?" Audrey asked, wishing she

could snatch back those words and throw them down her throat.

Bones smiled. "No, I don't have a girlfriend."

"Why not?" she asked.

"I guess I never found a girl who was worthy," he responded. "Or maybe I'm just too busy to give a woman the kind of time she might need."

"Damn, that's honest," Audrey said.

"It is what it is," he stated.

"Oh, make a right at the corner and my place is three houses down," Audrey instructed.

Bones pulled up in front of her house and shut off the engine. He got out and walked around the vehicle and opened Audrey's door for her. He then escorted her to her door. It was awkward for both as Audrey put the key in the door and unlocked it. Should she ask him in? After just meeting him? Did he expect to be asked in? What about a kiss?

Bones decided to take the lead and head back to his car after seeing her door open. He walked slowly back toward his car as he motioned good-bye. He had that enchanting no-teeth-showing smile on his face.

"Thank you for the ride," Audrey hollered.

Bones put his thumb and pinky up to his ear and mouthed "I'll call you" and got in his car and drove away.

Bones woke up with the sun, as he was accustomed to doing since he'd been a kid and had to deliver papers before school to make a few extra dollars. But this particular morning he woke up smiling, thinking about last night and Audrey. Bones wasn't the type of man who could fall for a woman quickly. It wasn't his style. In fact, he hadn't had a real girlfriend, ever. He considered it too much trouble.

"Women always get in the way with their drama," Bones shared with Juice one night on their way to a club. "Maybe when I'm fifty and finished hustling, I'll want to settle down for that bullshit."

Bones was preaching to the choir with Juice, whose motto was Bros Before Hoes."

He thought about that and smiled, too, because Bones felt himself changing, softening some. Maybe it was this new desire of his to get a degree. He'd contemplated enrolling for several years before he actually made his way into the classroom. The major step was prompted by Juice, who one week failed to pay Bones his usual three thousand dollars. When Bones asked him about it, Juice came down with a bout of amnesia, saying he had already paid him. They dealt in cash and there were no receipts. Bones decided not to argue about or press the issue. He wanted to believe that Juice had simply forgotten. But that incident made Bones realize that he was at the mercy of Juice's kindness, and he didn't like it.

Bones decided to make some changes. First, he saved a great deal of the money Juice did pay him, enough to purchase rental property. Then he decided to go back to school, taking classes at Hunter College toward a degree in accounting and business finance. He found that he had a knack for numbers. And succeeding in school gave him not only knowledge, but clarity and confidence.

Consumed by his pursuit of material possessions and fame, Juice didn't even notice the changes in Bones. Bones had always been quiet, so the distance that was growing between the two men was not discernible to Juice. But Bones knew.

Gone were the days when Bones and Juice spent a lot of time together because their mothers had disappeared on a drug binge. But their childhood secret and vow of friendship forced Bones to always come when Juice called, thus giving him no reason to ever doubt Bones's loyalty.

Bones studied a couple of hours for his Accounting II exam, which would be that Thursday. His simple Citizen watch read 10:00. Bones would never spend thousands on a watch, despite the ribbing from Juice.

"Man, when are you going to upgrade that watch of yours?"

Juice would say. "You can't be hanging with me with that cheap-ass watch. Get yourself a Rolex or one of those Jakob and Company's. I know I pay you enough."

"This watch tells the time," Bones would answer, unaffected by Juice's ribbing. "That's all it needs to do. Besides, you got enough diamonds and shit for the whole city of New York. I don't need to be seen. Everybody should be looking at you."

That seemed to make sense to Juice. Bones knew he could always appeal to his cousin's vanity. As he looked at his "cheap-ass" watch, he knew he had to get moving. He wanted to deal with Juice's business in Newark early. He wanted to get it out of the way so that it wouldn't ruin his evening. He decided to stop in East Orange first and collect his rents. That gave him encouragement and strength and kept his ultimate mission before him.

I'm just doing Juice's work until I have enough to never have to do his bidding.

No matter what time of year it was, the drab streets of Newark seemed unchanged in his old neighborhood. There was always litter in the streets and trash cans, overflowing with garbage, on the curb. The small houses appeared defeated, in need of much repair. Many of the projects had been torn down, but the despair and the depression of the spirit that resided in them had been carried to the next housing developments. In one of them was where Bones had to carry out his task.

"Here, Aunt Dee." Bones didn't really want to say hello. Just looking at her in her condition, still, after all these years, saddened him to his core.

"You're two days late," she accused, her hair doing its usual Don King/Medusa thing on top of her head.

"No, Aunt Dee," Bones protested. "Today is Tuesday. I always come on Tuesdays."

"It's Tuesday? It feels like Friday," Deidre said, motioning for Bones to come in. She used her foot to move some empty bottles and other trash out of the doorway.

"Nah, not today. I have to—," Bones started, trying to avoid another one of their tiresome talks.

"Get in here, boy!" she demanded. "I'm tired of you and James thinking y'all's too good for your mamas. How would you have felt if we were too busy for y'all coming up?"

The level of denial of drug addicts continually amazed Bones. Delusion had certainly set in. Juice hadn't been by or spoken a word to his mother since he'd graduated from high school and left for New York City.

Bones dragged his feet into the raggedy apartment. The room was dark and held no furniture. There were burn marks in the carpet, as if it had been used as an ashtray. A few nasty blankets were discarded on the floor. It looked very much like the place she'd had when he and Juice were boys.

Deidre led the way into the kitchen. She sat herself on top of an old milk crate she was using as a chair. She was skeleton thin and the crate was more than enough support.

"Aunt Dee, you need to use some of the money Juice sends you and get some furniture up in this joint," Bones said, still standing.

"Boy, don't you be telling me how to spend my money . . . my hush money," she said, breaking into a laugh, exposing her brownish gums. "I earned this!"

As the media attention started to settle on Juice and his mercurial rise within the music business, he'd had to create a story. Having a crackhead mother was played out and embarrassing. It was better to be an orphan, and the sympathy would come in handy. He wasn't worried about his mother crawling out of the woodwork to claim him. He knew she was too high even to pay attention. And when was she going to read *Vibe* or *Black Enterprise*? She didn't have cable, or even a television for that matter. The one they'd had when he was a kid was sold for a single hit of crack.

But once Juice started making serious money, either his guilt or his sense of duty kicked in and he started sending his mother money every week. His secret hope was that she might overdose, or get some bad drugs and die. That was his preference. But if she used it to pull herself out of her situation and off drugs, that was fine, too—just as long as she stayed in her place.

"Let that bitch know she doesn't have a son," Juice told Bones when he first started sending her money through him. "Let her know to keep her fucking mouth closed. Everybody thinks I'm an orphan, and as far as I'm concerned that's the honest-to-God truth. Just make sure she understands that, okay?"

No matter how bad Deidre and his mother were, Bones couldn't bring himself to call either names, not even behind closed doors. It was funny because he, too, was bitter because of what drugs had done to their lives, but they were still their mothers, Bones thought. He did what Juice asked him to do, though, and faithfully delivered the money along with the message.

Bones was frustrated watching Deidre live like this. Over the years, she had been given enough money to buy herself a home, a car, and whatever else she wanted or needed.

"I'm just saying you should use it for something more than crack," Bones slipped in.

"I don't use no drugs no more!" she protested. "I been clean two days now."

"Glad to hear it," Bones replied, humoring her. He knew that if she hadn't copped in a couple of days, it was because she had run through last week's money too fast. "Have you seen my mother?"

"Nah, it's be a long time since I seen Tawana," said Deidre, her eyes glassy. "I ask some people and ain't nobody seen her. That reminds me—some detectives came by the other day. They say they're looking into Benny's death. Can you believe that after all these years? I didn't even know he was dead. I mean, he just disappeared."

"Well, I better be headed out," responded Bones.

"Wait," Deidre stood up. "You tell James that I need to see him."

"Yeah, I'll tell him to come by," said Bones, leaning over to give Deidre a kiss on the forehead before walking out the door, knowing Juice would never come by.

Bones sat in his car for a moment or two. He thought about the night he and James had dragged the crackhead Benny to the Dumpster. A tear began to form in the corner of his eye as he realized how far away from that life he and Juice had traveled. Juice could just block things out of his mind as if they had never happened. But Bones held on to things as if they were a part of him.

They both had their virtues and vices, and influenced each other in unknowable ways. Bones knew that he would not be the person he was if it hadn't been for Juice, who'd looked out for him when he first started earning money. Bones had recognized a long time ago, though, that Juice wouldn't always be there to take care of him. If his childhood taught him nothing else, it taught him that everything could be upended in the blink of an eye. Bones had to take care of himself.

A few years before, while flipping through the channels on a Sunday morning, Bones caught a man on *Tony Brown's Journal* talking about wealth. Bones's ears perked up. The man had written a book called *The Hidden Cost of Being African American.* Bones sat there spellbound as the author broke down the reason blacks, even those with good-paying jobs and educations, were still far behind their white counterparts. From that point on, Bones had a different outlook on money.

At first he hoarded his money, keeping large amounts of cash in safes and boxes hidden all over his apartment. That was how the drug dealers he'd hung with had kept their money. It was all he knew.

But later, utilizing the expertise of a broker, he opened a mutual fund and started trading stocks and bonds regularly. He also bought two condos with cash on the cheap, in an up-and-coming building in East Orange, New Jersey, right off the parkway. He had rental dollars coming in every month in addition to the money Juice paid him and the thousands Juice would throw at him just because he'd gotten another bonus check from his clothing line or television deal.

Bones was a miser. He didn't spend money on jewelry, drove a simple American-made SUV, and stayed in one of his condos that was nearly paid off. Bones had the desire to have as much money as Juice. Whereas Juice splurged on lavish parties, expensive cars, and trips to exotic places, Bones would go along for the ride, but would only penny-pinch his own money. Tagging along with Juice, Bones traveled and ate for free. He got into every club for free, with VIP treatment. When everyone else was getting drunk and gambling, Bones sipped on club soda with a twist of lime. After everyone was pissy drunk, Bones would then look forward to the card games—easy money. Before long, Bones's frugality and wise investments gave him a net worth in the low millions. He was the kind of millionaire he'd always wanted to be—one nobody was checking on.

Bones met Juice at the studio. Lately, Juice had been driving Bones crazy with nerves over this new idea of his that he claimed he couldn't talk about over the phone. It was a secret project, and he needed Bones to arrange some last-minute details for it.

When Bones arrived at the studio, he found Juice and a few engineers sitting behind a massive keyboard, a far cry from the toy he'd enjoyed as a kid. Headphones over his ears, Juice was moving a few of the levers up and down, in a world of his own, while the other men, yawning, had their arms crossed behind their heads and their feet elevated on the furniture. Juice nodded his head back and forth rhythmically. When he caught sight of Bones, he removed the headphones and stood up as the other men took their feet off the furniture.

"Hey, Bones," Juice greeted him, putting his arm around Bones's shoulders and guiding him into a separate room. "Can you believe we been here all day waiting for that lame-ass Lil Red? I can't believe how late he is. Doesn't he know this studio time is costing *him*? He ain't even big time yet and he's fucking up."

"Some people believe the hype, man," Bones said, disinterested.

Last year, when Juice had gone to the Miami new music festival, he'd practically been attacked by this scrawny light-skinned kid with sandy-colored hair. Timothy Reddington, now known as Lil Red, had caught a bus from Jacksonville and had wormed his way into the event. The club was crowded and loud, but the kid didn't hesitate to perform. He spit out a rhyme in his slow, twangy drawl that hushed everyone in the immediate vicinity. Impressed by the kid's freestyling, Juice later gave him a recording contract.

"Remember when I signed him and he started spending the money before he left the Universal Building?" Juice laughed. "He went to the lobby and called his friend and booked him a flight so they could go shopping together. Then he bought that Range Rover."

Bones had to agree. "He's a dumb motherfucker! I don't even want to talk about him."

"Yeah, man, but the boy's CD is almost done," Juice said. "It's what we've all been working toward. His single has been selling through the roof. He might even be nominated for a Grammy in the best new artist category if we play our cards right."

"Like I said, I ain't even thinking about Lil Red," Bones emphasized.

"Man, you looking good. What you been up to?" Juice said with the joviality everyone loved.

"Oh, just maintaining. Just maintaining," Bones replied warming to Juice.

"Can I get you something to drink?"

"Nah, I'm good," answered Bones. "Ya moms got that old keyboard of yours and—"

Disinterested in anything to do with his mother, Juice cut Bones off.

"I asked you here because I have an important meeting coming up and I want you to make the arrangements."

"Not your assistant?" questioned Bones, while Juice motioned for the two of them to sit down.

"As I said on the phone, it's not really business-business, per se," Juice said. "I need someone I can trust fully, brick trust. Know what I mean?"

"Brick trust" was what Juice always said when he wanted Bones's complete attention and discretion. It was his way of bringing up the crackhead murder that had bound them and their loyalty to each other. Bones watched, mesmerized, as Juice went into the shopping list of details he needed Bones to take care of. Bones hadn't seen Juice this on edge about anything in a long time—not since he'd made his move to pull a coup at Universal Records so many years before.

"This is an odd bunch of stuff, man," commented Bones. "It ain't something for some of your homo friends, is it?"

"What are you talking about? Man, you know I don't get down like that. Homos make me sick," Juice said indignantly.

"Well, you know how I feel about that, especially given all we did to the crackhead."

"We?" Juice exclaimed.

"Man, don't even try to flip on—" Bones rose to his feet in anger.

"Nah, nothing like that," Juice said in a soothing voice, gesturing for Bones to sit back down. No matter how rich or powerful Juice became he knew that Bones could and would bust his ass if he got out of line.

"You know we're in this for life. You're my man and ain't nothing going to change that."

"Yeah . . . yeah, I know," Bones said with a little hesitation. "If you just tell me what this secret project is all about, I'm sure I can help you out more, cuz."

"In due time," Juice responded, "you'll know everything. I just need you to do me these solids. Don't I always take care of you?"

"I'ma handle things like I always do, Juice, but I don't like you keeping secrets from me," he said. "Not after all we've been through. You should feel like you can tell me anything."

Bones sat for a few seconds in silence, staring at his boots. He then looked Juice directly in the eyes.

"When you kill a man, it changes you, Juice," Bones said. "It changes you."

Bones got up and walked out. Getting on his assignment for Juice, Bones ran around the city picking up odd items—masquerade-type face coverings and gold keys for which he was instructed to purchase diamond-studded key chains.

Later that night he dropped everything off at Juice's mansion. Bones had never seen the record producer this elated. It was as if Juice were a rich kid in a toy store.

"You're going to love this. I have a huge surprise for you, Bones," said Juice, pleased with himself. "Here is the key to Club Eclipse. I bought it just for you!"

Desire creates the power.
—RAYMOND HOLLINGWELL

Chapter
10

Xavier was dressed in his navy blue power suit. He hated suits, but he figured that he didn't want to be too much of a renegade—at least not as seen from the door. A stickler for punctuality, he considered waiting until exactly eight, but he was too curious about the mysterious invitation he had received. He wanted to get there early, case the joint, and get a feel for what would go down. He was prepared for anything.

When he arrived at the address on the card, Xavier approached the concierge as instructed. The concierge left his post to personally escort Xavier, handing him a black gift bag that contained a fancy mask. He then asked Xavier to put it on.

He followed the older man in silence down a wood-paneled corridor lined with old, expensive paintings and tall antique vases. There was even a pedestal with a Fabergé egg on display under glass.

They made a left at the end of the hall, which appeared to lead to a dead end. The wall in front of him and the walls to the right and left were all identical, thick, heavy-framed dark wood.

"I believe the key you have, sir, should be used now," directed the concierge.

Xavier looked puzzled. Where was he supposed to use this key?

"There is a keyhole to your left," said the concierge. "You will have to feel for it. Once you find it, turn the key and an elevator will arrive to take you to your destination."

"Thank you," said Xavier to the man, who disappeared down the hall.

Xavier felt around the wall, and to his left, at eye level, was a small keyhole. He took the key out of his breast pocket and examined it. He inserted and turned the key and heard the hum of an engine coming to life. Shortly after, the wooden doors smoothly opened to reveal a leather-lined car. There were no buttons for selecting a floor. Xavier stepped into the elevator, the doors automatically closed, and the elevator began to move.

Xavier put the key back in his jacket pocket. It was a smooth ride, there were no sudden stops causing his stomach to rise up. Xavier felt his ears popping and swallowed hard to relieve the pressure.

The elevator finally came to a stop and the door opened onto a mahogany-lined foyer. Standing before him was a tall, slender black man dressed in a tuxedo. He also had on a mask, but more Batmanish than masquerade like Xavier's.

"You can put the key in that bowl," he said. "I will escort you to the meeting room."

The room was dimly lit, with candles lining a shelf that

spanned a half-mirrored wall in the back. On the other side of the room were a bar and a table next to it displaying hors d'oeuvres. There were masked servers behind each post. Xavier walked over to the huge black granite conference table. There were four plush leather seats on one side of the table and three on the other. There was a thronelike seat at the head. On the table, in front of each seat, was a gold key that hung from a diamond tennis bracelet, and a business card, a plain black business card with no writing on it.

Before Xavier had an opportunity to explore his environment further, he was startled by the sound of an old grandfather clock. The chimes were followed by the *cling, cling, cling* of what he knew to be other keys dropping in the glass bowl. Six men in masks similar to Xavier's marched into the room. They all stood in silence looking at one another for a second, then they heard a muffled, yet authoritative, voice: "Gentlemen, please take a seat."

A man, also wearing a mask and a dark, hooded cloak, stood at the head of the table. After the other six men took their seats, the one in the robe ceremoniously took his.

"Welcome to the initiation meeting of the Seven Figures Club," the cloaked man began. "I want to thank you all for accepting this invitation. You have been hand-selected from among the many thousands of national leaders, captains of industry, entertainment giants, and media moguls to be part of a unique opportunity.

"I'm certain many of you have read about groups such as the Masons and the Illuminati. And perhaps you thought they were myths, these groups of men who literally rule the world and shape history. Seven Figures will be that kind of group. At the very least we will rule our own individual worlds.

"Together—with our collective contacts, access to money and media, our collective drive and vision—we will be able to not only control one another's destiny, but if we play our cards right, our impact will be even greater. But first, let's go over *our* wildest dreams. These are the things the Seven Figures can make happen in your life. We can make you an owner of an NBA franchise, we can secure you a seat on the Federal Reserve, we can make you the president of the United States . . ."

Xavier tuned everything out after he heard the words "an NBA franchise." This man at the head of the table was speaking directly to him, as Xavier imagined the other goals directly related to other men at the table. He was impressed by the idea of being in a secret club with a future president. Xavier could tell by the shifting of the other men in their seats that they were becoming eager, too, by just contemplating their potential higher level of power.

"Now, gentlemen, everyone in this room works very hard. That's one of the many reasons you were selected. But if you work hard, you have to play hard, too. Being a Seven Figures member will entitle you to personal rewards as well. Before you are a key and a card. The card will get you into the VIP section of the hottest nightclub in New York, Club Eclipse. With this card, you will have free drinks and other *satisfying* perks that the club has to offer.

"The key is a skeleton key. It opens many locks, including the doors to the private back rooms at the Club Eclipse. These back rooms will allow you to enact your most secret personal desires. They come fully equipped with whatever items *or persons* with whom you want to share intimate time. If our information is correct, which I've done the research to ensure, you will not be disappointed."

Xavier fingered the key. He felt as if he was playing *Dungeons & Dragons* or something similar.

"Finally, men, I warn you that this is a lifetime membership." The cloaked man's tone had turned from jovial to ominous. "There is only one way into the Seven Figures and there will be only one way out. If you decide to become a member, which you have to do tonight or forever walk away, you must make a commitment in blood to swear to honor the bonds that we create and to keep confidential all of our dealings. Members will sign the contract I have here."

He waved a black piece of paper featuring gold writing.

"If you decide not to be a part of this group at the end of our discussion, you may simply leave the room."

"What do you mean there is only one way out?" Xavier asked.

"Death," responded the leader. "Once you sign that contract, you will be a member for life—till death do us part, if you will."

"Are you serious?" another man at the table asked.

"We cannot expect to accomplish the things I've talked about in this room without everyone participating and keeping it confidential. Anyone is more than welcome to walk out of this place and never again think about the Seven Figures. The choice is yours."

"How do we know the club will come through for us?" a different man asked.

"You don't know. This will be your first test. You will have to trust us as we will have to trust one another."

The cloaked man passed around the contract. One by one, each man read it. The first reader started to reach for a pen.

"No, don't sign yet. We'll get to that," said the man at the head of the table.

The first man passed the contract on to the next who also read it and passed it on. The third, after reviewing the words on the page, stood up, walked toward the door, and left. No one said a word. Next, Xavier examined the contract, which expressed the necessity of discretion and the ways in which the men would be protected. It also stated that the cost of membership was one million dollars annually. Xavier was tempted to leave, but his desire to own an NBA team kept him in his seat. He passed the contract on to the next person. After the contract made its way to the head of the table, there were six remaining invitees.

A masked servant entered the room carrying a small crystal bowl. He placed it next to the group's organizer.

"We shall now sign in blood," the cloaked man announced.

The servant made his way around the room. He wiped each man's finger with an alcohol swab, and pricked each man's finger with a needle taken from a sealed package. He drained a few droplets of blood into the bowl from each man, including the leader. Then, the leader circulated the contract, this time giving each invitee a fountain pen to dip into the bowl and use to write his signature on the contract. Xavier was eager to see the names on the list when the contract was placed in front of him, but the dimness of the room and the red blood on black paper made it indecipherable.

When the contract made its way back around to the head of the table, he, too, signed.

"Men, you may now remove your masks."

Xavier was stunned by the company he was keeping. The only member he knew personally was Carl. The others were men he had only seen pictures of in newspapers and in *Fortune* magazine. Xavier strutted over to Carl as the men began to socialize, enjoying the food and drink.

"The game was great the other night," exclaimed Xavier, trying to make small talk rather than tackle the mysterious commitment he had just made.

Ignoring the sports talk, Carl said, "I hope we're not in over our heads. I thought about walking out with that other guy, but I just had to know who else was invited to join this group. I'm happy I stayed. Just look at this roster of power brokers."

Xavier scanned the room again as Carl pointed people out to him.

There was James Lamar Kennedy, Juice, the most powerful man in entertainment, talking in one corner to Senator Dustin Hernandez from the state of California.

"It's the Seven Figures," Dustin proclaimed. "I know I signed my name and everything, but I'm getting nervous. What if it gets out that I'm part of some clandestine group? Everything that I've worked so hard for will be ruined."

"Dustin, Dustin, Dustin. You worry too much," Juice said, calmly taking another sip of his martini. "No one will find out. Only the men in this room know about this group and there are certain safeguards we have in place. Please don't worry."

The senator was a bona fide sex symbol. He was a bigger version of Mark Consuelos, Kelly Ripa's husband, and had a similar charisma and quick wit, which made him a beast during debates. Senator Hernandez had won over the constituents in California when he was able to quell the gang violence in Los Angeles and bring economic empowerment to Watts, Compton, and South Central.

In this room, also, was Renard Rooks. Carl informed Xavier that the esteemed lawyer was his fraternity brother and that they had crossed over at the same time and shared a branding on their left thighs to prove it.

"We decided to put our brands somewhere where no one else

would see it," Carl said to Xavier. "I guess we were preparing for this secret even back then."

Carl went on to explain that Renard was a quiet and reserved man who had made a name for himself representing high-profile legal cases. He had gotten a criminal off who was standing with a machete in his hand over a hacked-up murder victim when the police busted in—or so people said. He was a ruthless man without a conscience, the one Machiavelli might have had in mind when he warned, "Keep your friends close; keep your enemies closer."

From the movie side, there was Griffin Mallory. He was an outspoken, over-the-top movie executive. He loved making headlines and didn't bite his tongue. Griffin wanted to be bigger than the Weinsteins and Spielberg. He also wanted to eliminate the negative images of black men that dominated the movies.

"I'm tired of seeing black men always playing thugs and villains," he'd said during one of his interviews. "And if I see one more black man dressed up like a fat black woman, I'm going to kill somebody!"

Another invitee, Rex Longfellow, had followed his father into the ministry, much the way Adam Clayton Powell Jr. and Martin Luther King Jr. had followed their respected reverend dads. Like Powell and King, Rex used his ministry to make waves politically and socially. He'd created a wealth movement within his ministry that saw his following grow from several hundred to almost a quarter of a million within five years. After studying under Bishop Branch Howard, Rex had broken away and gone out on his own. He was now the leader of one of the largest mega churches in the country, which the Seven Figures leader promised to triple, with satellite churches in every major state.

"Gentlemen, one last thing," Juice said.

The servers circulated around the room with silver trays containing iPhones.

"This is your Seven Figures phone. It is encrypted and unhackable. You will be text-messaged and contacted about meetings and meeting places, updates, and news of our progress. Please keep this phone with you at all times because you never know when you will be contacted. Please also keep it on Vibrate. And, fellas, don't let it get into the hands of your ladies. You may be sloppy in your private lives, if you like. But this no longer is about you. You are responsible to each man in this room. Keep it tight for all of our sakes."

"I am looking forward to making history with you all!"

Juice exited the room, permitting the men to mingle freely.

Once Juice left the room, he headed down the hall, through
the study and to a hidden room behind a false wall. This
was a sort of "panic room," with all of the technology and security features and luxury to match with its comfortable plush
leather seating, satellite and short-circuit radio, and television.

Mortimer Zane had been there for more than an hour,
observing the entire meeting from this room. Witnessing his
protégé command such dominance over some of the most influential men in the country gave him a hard-on. He was massaging
his member, making the blood from his body rush to meet his
fingertips.

The orchestrator of the Seven Figures sauntered in with a
confidence that was both sexy and scary. Juice stood at six one
and had the complexion of the actor Morris Chestnut. He had

deep-set dark brown eyes that seemed to be able to penetrate steel. His physique was muscular, but not beefy. He worked out twice a week to maintain this, but he could easily have had the perfect body if he'd devoted more time to it.

Juice stopped in front of Mortimer, leaning over the silver-haired man, his hands balancing on the arms of the chair, within inches of Mortimer's face.

"So how did I do?" Juice asked in a voice just above a whisper.

"You were a monster. I'm incredibly proud of you," said Mortimer, elated.

"Yeah, but what about Nick Chamberlain, who decided *not* to join. We're going to need that judge and his connections. Who are we going to replace him with?"

Mortimer didn't respond with words, instead he reached out and grabbed both sides of Juice's face and kissed him hard and passionately. Juice welcomed his touch. He had been waiting for this kind of release. All that talk of money and power, all that testosterone swirling around the room, mixing with expensive cologne, had completely aroused Juice. Mortimer reached underneath Juice's cloak, deftly unzipped the slightly baggy Brooks Brothers steel gray suit pants to release Juice's thick eight and a half inches. His penis bounced out like a tight diving board. Mortimer dived in face-first.

Juice's knees almost buckled as Mortimer went to work on the tip of his penis, licking, sucking, and squeezing softly all at the same time. Juice looked down to see Mortimer on his knees before him. His thin lips were stretched around his dick with a hunger that made Juice grow another half an inch.

Juice closed his eyes. He wanted to drink in each sensation. Juice moaned, which only encouraged Mortimer. Never taking his mouth off Juice's dick and sucking his balls simultaneously, Mortimer managed to stick his pointer and middle fingers into Juice's ass. It was unexpected, both the action and the reaction. When Mortimer hit that spot, deep inside Juice, he shot his load almost immediately into Mortimer's mouth and all over his face, collapsing with his pants still around his ankles and the cloak covering most of his body.

Juice and Mortimer pulled themselves together and entered another wing of Mortimer's expansive apartment. Juice took a shower in the master bath, then rejoined Mortimer.

Juice tightened the belt around his black silk robe. He was in the bedroom looking out of one of the floor-to-ceiling windows of Mortimer Zane's penthouse apartment. Collectively, the windows offered a panoramic view of New York City—a view few got to see. It was beyond the view Juice had imagined more than twenty years before when he'd vowed to be rich. He had arrived at a place in life exceeding his expectations.

In this Fifth Avenue apartment, Juice was forty-five floors up and casting his eyes over the most powerful and influential city in the world. And he was one of the most powerful and influential men in this city. Juice felt as if he was literally on top of the world.

"You like this view, huh?" asked Mortimer, seemingly coming from out of nowhere.

"Yeah, I like it a lot."

"Well, all this can be yours, you know," Mortimer said.

"It is mine," Juice replied with a chuckle.

"Not quite yet," Mortimer warned. "Don't get ahead of yourself."

"Weren't you the one to tell me that I must claim what I want?"

"Yes, but you might want some humility and reality to go with that audacity," Mortimer chided. "Don't forget where you came from."

The last thing Juice wanted to do was remember where he came from. All of the memories he had spent two decades erasing were threatening to resurface.

"What's got your forehead all knotted up, Juice?" Mortimer asked as he snapped the band closed on his Rolex. "Let me guess. You're not sure if you had sex with me for pleasure or for power, right?"

"I don't know what the fuck to think. But that's pretty close," said Juice, never taking his eyes off the spectacular New York skyline.

Every time Juice had sex with a man he was reminded of Benny the crackhead. Even though it had been unwelcome at such an early age, the demented drug addict was the first person to show Juice how a man's body could be pleasured. He had revealed to Juice parts of his body he was not even completely aware of. And when Benny did so and performed certain unmentionable acts, Juice discovered a particular pleasure, although undesired at the time. Afterward, Juice always felt miserable. A routine he had come to associate with sex—feeling amazingly good during the act, then painfully bad after it. It made sex confusing, yet habitual, like a mind-numbing drug.

"You know, if you take the emotion out of sex, it's just a release—you're just getting your shit off," Mortimer explained. "I just happened to be a powerful man who you fucked. It doesn't make you a fag. That's what men do. We fuck! You just happened to have fucked a powerful man, so that makes you a 'fucking' genius!"

Mortimer broke into laughter as he left the bedroom.

Juice had known this man for only a year and a half. In this short time, through Mortimer's contacts, Juice had gone from a record-company executive in the black music department to owning his own label, signing a television deal, and making plans to create his own clothing line. He was currently in talks with a Hollywood bigwig to produce a few films. In addition, he was building his financial portfolio, under Mortimer's guidance. Juice was learning to move away from what he called "acting niggerish"—spending his money on "depreciating" assets, such as rental homes in the Hamptons, cars, jewelry, and clothes, and in some cases, women. Certain things were harder to break from than others.

Mortimer was revealing the secrets that few men like Juice ever get to know—no matter how wealthy they became. It was knowledge that made one powerful, not money.

Mortimer Zane was a mysterious man. His name was not found on any *Forbes* or *Fortune 500* lists because he paid handsomely *not* to be there. But he was, in fact, the third-wealthiest man in the world. He didn't need the world to know how rich he was as long as *he* knew it. He had holdings in untraceable offshore accounts. He'd made most of his fortune through real estate. His initial investment, however, had come from other kinds of deals, but he'd parlayed that money into bricks and mortar, something his father had taught him.

"You will always be wealthy as long as you have property," Mortimer's father told him when Mortimer was fifteen. "Food, clothing, and shelter are the three staples of life. But only shelter can build equity."

It was a mantra that he lived by and shared with a small group of his select friends.

Mortimer bought his first building in Manhattan when real estate there was in the dumps. Over the course of five years he acquired a whole neighborhood in a section then called Hell's Kitchen. At the time, it was overrun with crime, prostitution, and drugs. Now it boasted some of the most exclusive luxury apartment buildings and was even home to a few major media outlets.

But he did not stop there. Quietly, Mortimer bought up large portions of New York City, under different corporate names. Unlike Donald Trump, whose ego seemed to demand that he put his name on everything in huge, gaudy brass letters, Mortimer put his name on nothing. He liked being able to walk the streets and even on occasion take the subway or go to Washington Square Park without being recognized. There were few articles written about him because he didn't grant interviews. Few knew how far this man's tentacles reached or exactly where he'd come from or what he was about.

Mortimer had more money than he could ever spend in his lifetime. What motivated him was having control and using his power. Mortimer liked having an idea and seeing it come to fruition on a large scale, affecting the lives of millions. He loved picking up a paper or turning on CNN and seeing an event unfold and knowing that he had had something to do with it.

"There is nothing you can't have," Mortimer said to Juice. "And I want to help you get it. You have drive *and* charisma. I always had the drive, but never the charisma. Together we can do a lot."

"So I'm more than someone you can explore your deepest thoughts and fantasies with?" Juice said, rubbing his chin.

"Yes, you are more to me," Mortimer said, leaning in with a father's protective stance.

Juice sat down, comforted by the sense of security Mortimer extended with the tone of his voice.

"You are real, much better than the phony jokers of the country-club crowd who compare their investments, their homes, and their wives as if they are making up for what they lack inside," Mortimer said. "They're always trying to live up to some image of what they think they should be, and most of the time it is just a lie."

Juice felt a sudden coldness in the room, as if Mortimer was talking to someone else. There was distance in his sharp words. Juice stood up and walked across the room. Mortimer followed him over to the window and continued to talk, this time drawing Juice back in by the subject.

"Wealth and money isn't enough," Mortimer said. "Money can't make you cool, or buy you a personality or a soul. It can't give you substance. And it certainly doesn't bring you fun or happiness. I'm happy and having fun for the first time in a long while. You have brought that to me."

Juice smiled with his usual youthful exuberance, but his smile contained an exciting street edge. He thought about his own ability to turn a simple deal into a blockbuster and the praise he received from Mortimer when he did so. Now his biggest accomplishment to date was starting the Seven Figures Club, a secret society of powerful men who he hoped would eventually rule the world.

Juice was obsessed with and fascinated by talk of the Skull and Bones and the Illuminati. He read about secret organizations such as the Masons, of which supposedly everyone who signed the Declaration of Independence was a member. He heard that every president was a Mason or a member of the Skull and Bones and that the Illuminati had a plan for a New World Order that would have everyone at their mercy. Juice wanted a piece of that action. He wanted to control at least his corner of the universe and be able to truly map out his own destiny. He never wanted to be vulnerable again.

A FEW WEEKS LATER

New York City to Miami, Florida

Juice handed Woodrow a hundred-dollar bill and stepped out of the town car and onto the tarmac, ready to board his private jet, a Gulfstream. It was better than any Bentley, any May-bach, any Ferrari he had ever owned. His jet brought him true peace and freedom. It had been a few years since he'd flown commercially and he didn't miss it. Even in first class, he had to deal with people recognizing him. The last straw was when he was boarding a plane for the Grammys and the flight was de-layed. For two hours he must have signed more than a thousand autographs, and it did not stop—not even in midair.

To avoid the traffic to the larger airports, he flew out of Teterboro, where with a day's notice his plane would be gassed up and ready to go anywhere in the United States and parts of Europe. The plane accommodated fourteen people, but on this

trip it was just Juice and Bones, like old times. Juice had scheduled a trip to Miami, deciding to kill two birds with one stone:
He had to deal with Senator Dustin Hernandez, who wanted to
discuss his involvement in the Seven Figures Club; and there was
a new music seminar where he wanted to check out a vocalist
from New York who had industry buzz.

"Yo, cuz, I can't wait to touch down in Miami," said Bones as
he got comfortable in his plush leather seat. "You know I love
the Delano!"

"Especially the penthouse suite, right?" Juice said.

Juice and Bones had started their hustle in junior high. Juice,
who was a master deejay, threw parties and Bones provided the
security and collected the money. They made enough to keep
Juice in clean clothes throughout high school—most of the
time.

"I can't believe that we're here for only three days," said
Bones. "Next time we come back, I'm looking for a place down
here."

"That sounds good," replied Juice, looking at his iPhone and
the text that Dustin had sent him about his arrival time.

"So, you have an additional iPhone?" asked Bones. "What's
up? You don't trust me after all these years?"

Normally, Bones answered Juice's calls and text messages.

"Now, you know I trust you with my life," Juice responded.
"This is . . . well, a bit sensitive. I already told you that I have a lot
of people depending on this thing staying a secret. While I know
you will never tell a soul, I want to set a good example."

"I understand," Bones said, slightly irritated.

They flew the rest of the way to Miami in silence. Juice
flipped through back issues of *Vibe* and *Rolling Stone* and Bones
read *A Separate Peace* for one of his classes.

The flight landed smoothly. Bones knelt down and crossed himself and kissed the ground, a ritual after every flight.

"Man, come on with that shit," Juice pleaded.

"Fuck you, I'm giving praise," Bones said.

"That's some old *stupid*-stition." Juice chuckled.

"It may be, but I ain't never died on a plane yet and I do it before and after every flight," said Bones.

"Well, I ain't never died on a flight and I don't do that stupid shit," Juice responded. "I hope you catch herpes or something kissing the nasty ground like that!"

"Man, why you so cold?" Bones remarked. "You can't be wishing herpes on a brother like that. And if you do wish it on me, let it be from me eating some of the best coochie in the world."

"Yeah, like that woman you been seeing?" Juice grinned. "What's her name again?"

"Oh, don't even go there!" Bones said, getting serious. "And it's Audrey. Show some respect."

"Don't let me find out you're falling for some woman."

Bones was quiet.

They stopped off at the Delano, dropped their bags, and headed to the first night of the two-day new music seminar. They pulled up in a chauffer-driven Mercedes and bypassed the ropes, going straight into the VIP section. No lists needed to be checked. Juice Kennedy was the most important man in the room.

The liquor was flowing steadily all night. After two acts had gone up, the anxious Juice was ready to go.

"I need to get out of here," Juice said to Bones.

"But we haven't seen who we came to see," Bones protested.

"I'll hear her some other time," Juice said. "If she's that good, she'll be around."

Bones cut a path through the crowd for Juice. As they were making their way to the door, a young woman took the stage. She looked like a young Dorothy Dandridge. She had on a halter dress that showed off her thin but muscular arms and sexy cleavage. She looked timid and demure, but when she opened her mouth, she instantly silenced the entire club. The first few notes were like those of a siren, paralyzing all who heard. She had a rare, extraordinary voice, a cross between the sweetness of Tamia and the raspy strength of an early Whitney Houston. Juice was just a few feet from the door, but he stopped dead in his tracks.

"She sounds like an angel," Bones said.

"And she looks like one, too," replied Juice, stunned.

Juice had never believed in love at first sight because he'd never believed in love. But he was feeling something unfamiliar and her name was Brianna Banks.

Lately, Juice had been trying to move away from the music game and concentrate more on his profitable clothing line and film interests. Young people purchasing one song online, rather than entire CDs, were causing record companies to see a huge decline in sales. But listening to Brianna had given him renewed hope. He imagined that he could use her voice to turn her into a contemporary Diana Ross/Whitney Houston/Tina Turner. Brianna's voice was honest talent, and he knew from experience that the real thing always sells. If Juice signed Brianna, he would be able to leave the game on top. She could be his swan song.

When Brianna walked off the stage, Juice and Bones were waiting for her behind the curtain. Juice was seductive, telling her how he would work with her personally and make her a household name.

"We haven't had a real diva since Diana Ross—one who could

cross over, do movies, stay in the game for forty years. You will be the one," he told her.

Juice and Bones slipped out of the club and returned to the Delano. The producer couldn't stop thinking about that beautiful songbird. He even liked the way her name rolled off his tongue, *Brianna Banks.*

"Yo, cuz!" Bones said. "I know you better sign this girl ASAP."

"Done deal," Juice replied. "You find her manager and have him come talk to us. Put that in my schedule."

Juice felt his iPhone vibrate. It was a text message from Dustin asking when they could meet. Juice responded:

> 2-morrow at 7 at your hotel.
> What's ur room no.? I don't want
> anyone to see me.

What's your secret business again?" Bones asked, folding his arms over his chest.

"I'll let you in on it soon enough, cuz," said Juice, recognizing Bones's irritation.

Juice turned in for the night with Brianna's voice playing over and over in his head.

Juice got up at six the next morning. He showered and put on his sweats, trying to look as regular—read, unrecognizable—as possible. He left from a side entrance and down the street caught a cab. He was at Dustin's by ten to seven. He tapped lightly on the room door. Dustin opened it almost immediately.

"Thanks for coming," said Dustin, offering Juice some coffee and a bagel. "Do you want me to order you breakfast?"

"Nah, I don't eat breakfast," Juice replied. "But I will have some of your OJ if you don't mind."

Juice poured himself a glass and took a sip.

"So . . . what's on your mind?" asked Juice, not wanting to waste any time on chitchat.

"It's the Seven Figures. In thinking things over, I think the risks may be too high for me," Dustin started.

"You didn't fly all this way to tell me that you're getting cold feet," Juice said. "What is it, really?"

Dustin didn't speak for a moment. He wasn't at a loss for words, but was at a loss as to how to word his problem.

"Out with it," Juice commanded.

"I've done some things in my past," Dustin began hesitantly. "I have some skeletons in my closet. I was wondering if you could help me get rid of the bones."

"You mean the young man you were taking care of in South Central?"

"How did you—" Dustin was in shock.

"Dustin, we know everything," Juice interrupted. "Don't worry—that will never get out. That young man will not be any trouble to you. It will be taken care of. Not only that, at Club Eclipse there will be someone new for you. Someone you'll never have to call a skeleton."

"How? What—"

"Don't ask," Juice said. "Just know, like I said, that membership has its privileges. We take care of our own. You're part of a family now."

Juice drained the last of his orange juice and walked over to Dustin, sitting at the table next to him. He took the man by the hand and led him to his bedroom. Dustin didn't protest but was both puzzled and nervous.

He gently guided Dustin to the bed and had him sit down. Juice stood in front of him and undid the drawstring of his sweatpants and let them drop to the floor.

"I'm going to take care of your problem," Juice said. "But I need you to take care of my little, well, big problem."

Juice held his thick manhood in his hand and presented it to Dustin, who paused a moment. Juice had the thickest hunk of meat Dustin had ever laid eyes on in person. It was chocolate-covered perfection, and the head, that head was so big it looked like a giant spongy mushroom.

"I see why they call you Juice," was all Dustin could say as he licked his lips, his own hard-on trapped beneath his pants.

"So are you just going to sit there and admire this? Or are you going to take care of daddy?"

Dustin took care of daddy. He took care of daddy better than daddy expected.

J uice got back to the hotel before Bones had gotten up. Bones found Juice in the living room of their suite, whistling and reading the paper, when he came out of his bedroom.

"Boy, you're in a good mood," Bones said. "Good to see. You must have had a good night's sleep thinking about Brianna. So you ready to go back to New York and take on the world?"

"More than ready, cuz," Juice replied. "More than ready!"

LaJuan and Jacob were outside Club Eclipse, the hottest new nightclub in New York. They walked past the long line of plebes waiting for their turn to be rejected or accepted. Club Eclipse was one of those selective places. If you did not have the right look, you did not get in. As Jacob and LaJuan waited for the security guard behind the velvet rope to find LaJuan's name on the VIP guest list, at least a dozen people were turned away.

"Are you sure your name's on that list?" Jacob asked nervously. "I would hate to do that walk of shame."

"Oh relax," LaJuan said. "You're with me tonight. I know you're a little out of your element, but you have to be cool. You ain't never missed a week of classes, and you always be doing what your moms tells you. Now that you're on your own, you don't know what to do, huh? Just tell me, does that credit card she gave you and pays for say 'Momma's Boy'?"

LaJuan laughed all the way into the club.

The atmosphere inside Club Eclipse was wild. It was something out of an Usher or Puffy video. The baseline was thumping loud enough to make the room feel as if it was shaking. There were half-clad women in cages and shirtless men on top of the giant speakers, moving to the music. Everyone on the dance floor seemed to be choreographed zombies—bouncing their bottoms and waving their arms—hypnotized by the rhythm.

This was Jacob's first time in a club. His parents only permitted their son to use his recreational time at cultural and artistic events, where he would best have the opportunity to make the proper social connections. In their opinion, clubs were a haven for trouble, places where the wrong element could be found doing drugs, drinking alcohol, and having sex.

Fascinated by the sense of abandon the dancers demonstrated, Jacob felt his adrenaline rushing. He had never seen anything like this. He'd had no idea what he had been missing. He was spellbound, like a tourist from Iowa in New York City's Time Square.

"What's wrong with you, man?" LaJuan yelled over the music. "I swear you're acting like you're foreign, like you're from another country."

Jacob felt like an extra in a Broadway show. He couldn't take his eyes off all the gyrating bodies. He began to move right along with them, seduced by the best. He watched a woman slide down a pole from the second level of the club to the first.

"Please close your mouth, man," said LaJuan as he parted the crowd to make his way to the back of the club.

A tall Asian man stood in front of the rope that separated the

VIP section from the rest of the club. He didn't even acknowledge the two young men standing in front of him—that was, until LaJuan pulled out a black card.

The business-size card had no words on it, only two small raised dots in the upper-left-hand corner. As if he read Braille, the Asian man ran his fingers over the dots, then moved the rope to allow LaJuan and Jacob to walk through.

Behind the rope was a curtain. In back of the curtain were four private booths. LaJuan and Jacob sat down in one of them. Jacob felt important as the clubgoers walked by, noticeably taking a look at him and his friend simply because they were sitting in the VIP section. A woman placed a stand with champagne on ice next to Jacob and LaJuan's booth.

"Did she bring that for us?" asked Jacob.

"Yeah, man. Pass me a glass," said LaJuan, taking a swig, then leaning back as if he owned the place.

Jacob also got comfortable as the alcohol began to flow through him.

"I ain't trying to sit here all night, man," said Jacob as he made his way out of the booth.

"Nah, I'm chillin'," responded LaJuan, pulling out his cell. "I'm not trying to do all that moving and sweating just yet. I'm here for business."

Jacob made his way out onto the dance floor. It didn't take two minutes before he found himself sandwiched between two women. After eight straight songs, Jacob was drenched and thirsty. He made his way back to the VIP section. When he got to his booth, a man was sitting with LaJuan.

Rather than disturb the two, Jacob went over to the bar.

Earlier that evening, Jacob was bored. He had been hanging in his apartment doing nothing ever since he'd stopped going to classes. When LaJuan entered the living room dressed to go out, Jacob saw it as his opportunity for excitement. LaJuan agreed to Jacob joining him, but he couldn't interfere in his business. Now, in their booth, business was taking place. The man sitting with LaJuan looked familiar. Jacob remembered him from the Garden when they'd caught the Knicks game in Carl's skybox.

Bones leaned into LaJuan, close enough to not be overheard.

"See, I'm looking for an elite group of young men, for some events that we will be throwing here and around the world periodically," Bones began. "I need some dudes who have that look, who know how to carry themselves, who have that personality, you know what I mean?"

LaJuan nodded.

"You will always have to be on time for your assigned destination and you must always be impeccably groomed," Bones continued. "Basically, you'll be running your own business, so you need to treat the whole situation like a business. The minute you fuck up, you will be removed. What you see and what you hear while on business is not to be repeated to anyone. If you are found to have been out there talking to *anyone* about what you do or what you see, you will be dealt with.

"Now if you can abide by all that, this can be a really lucrative experience. You can set yourself up for life if you keep your head right. I'm discussing this with you LaJuan because I see that you like nice things. You are also educated and presentable. You can make conversation and look good doing it."

Bones's cell rang. He held a finger up to LaJuan.

"Hey, lady," Bones said, his demeanor softening. "I miss you, too."

Bones took the phone from his ear, reached into his pocket, and tossed five crisp hundred-dollar bills on the table. Addressing LaJuan, Bones said, "I'll give you a call soon with your next gig. Enjoy yourself. "

"Word," said LaJuan.

"It's just an artist . . . ," Bones said into his phone while walking away.

LaJuan left a hundred on the table and scooped up the rest of the money. He took half a step, then turned and picked up the hundred replacing it with a ten. He strutted over to the bar to get Jacob.

"Drink up, man," LaJuan said. "We have to bounce."

"Where're we headed?" asked Jacob. "I'm just starting to get my party on."

"We got a pocketful of lap dances to get!" LaJuan pulled out the money to show Jacob.

"You made money that fast, LaJuan? You definitely got to let me in on this," pleaded Jacob.

Take that from the top, Brianna!" Juice yelled into the intercom from the other side of the glass. "I need you to go up on that last note and no riffs. Save that shit for the concert tour."

Brianna belted out the tune just the way Juice had told her to. It was the sweetest sound he'd ever heard. He was mesmerized watching Brianna, who had her eyes closed, feeling every note.

"That was perfect," Juice whispered under his breath. It was his style to rarely compliment his artists. He didn't want them to get too comfortable and think they were good enough. He wanted them to keep striving for perfection. But for the first time in his career, Juice thought he might actually have heard perfection. Brianna had recorded six songs in a row and her voice on the last one was as strong and as beautiful as on the first.

Juice told Brianna to take a fifteen-minute break. There was a piano in another soundproof room adjacent to where she was doing her vocals. She grabbed a bottled water from the waiting area between rooms and headed into the room with the piano. She sat at the piano and started playing. Getting into a song that she had written, she hummed as she played. Her intensity reminded Juice of himself as a young boy, the way he'd played in his room with his beloved keyboard. The purity of her skills inspired Juice. In the control room, Juice worked out something on the boards with the engineer.

"Does that song have words?" asked Juice through the intercom.

"Um, yes," said Brianna, a little startled, not knowing he could hear her.

"Gerry, turn the recorder on," Juice commanded as he left the studio and headed into the room where Brianna was.

"Can you sing that song for me?" Juice asked Brianna.

Brianna grinned and began to sing, glancing up periodically to look deeply into Juice's eyes. Against his will he felt his heart skip a beat.

I'm looking in your eyes
I see a bright sunrise.
Your dreams are as big as mine,
Please come home with me tonight.
May tonight turn into forever,
The days will be seamless when we're together.
You make me forget the pain of my past,
No one can tell me our love isn't meant to last.

It required only one take. That song would go on Brianna's CD just as they had recorded it impromptu.

"Okay, Brianna, that's a wrap for today," Juice announced. For the first time in his adult life, Juice felt uneasy, out of control. Beginning to sweat, all he could think about was getting out of there. Her lyrics were powerful and seemed directed at him.

"We have eight more songs to do," Brianna protested.

"But we can stop for now. Go home and rest your voice and I'll see you tomorrow," Juice responded.

Normally Juice would have made Brianna, in one night, do every song that he wanted on her CD. It was his way to torture his artists, just to see what they were made of, and he loved to see them break. But, in this case, Brianna was breaking him.

In the past, he had not met a woman who did not in some way remind him of his mother. Brianna was different. There was nothing about her that indicated she had ever been used or abused. She showed no scars from life—not while she was performing anyway, not the side Juice had seen. She displayed a refreshing optimism about life. There wasn't even a hint of desperation.

Brianna stood close in front of Juice. She was fearless where his personal boundaries were concerned. In unfamiliar territory, he began to back away. She reached for one of his hands. She held two of his fingers in her right hand and two in her left, the way a child would hold hands and bask in the joy of a father's love.

Please, please, her eyes beamed up at him as she swung his arms back and forth.

Juice didn't know what to make of her behavior, but her innocence struck something deep in his heart.

"Okay, one more," he said, letting out a small laugh to ease his tension.

"I get to sing another song, I get to sing another song," she chanted as she skipped back into the recording room.

Juice was completely enthralled as he observed Brianna performing an upbeat song. She swung her head from side to side with the lightness of a woman not burdened by life. She shook her hips in a jerky motion that only made Juice laugh.

Who was this woman?

After the song Brianna collected her things and was ready to leave. Juice watched her pick up her bag and was turned on by the way her hair hung along her neckline as she bent over. Her body was banging, even in the loose-fitting khakis and oversize shirt she wore. She seemed completely unaware of her sex appeal.

"Thank you, Juice, for believing in me," she said.

Juice just stood there. Brianna had in that moment robbed him of the pain of his past, as well as of his words.

Juice's usual response would be to flirt, but he was reluctant to do this. There was something about her that made him want to behave himself. He didn't even want to kiss her good-bye when she placed her cheek near his mouth for the typical industry salutation. Instead he stood there and drank in the smell of her Chanel No. 5—an old-school scent for such a young woman—and the scent of aloe in her unprocessed long hair. She stepped away as he remained frozen, teetering on his desire.

"See you tomorrow," she said.

"No, no, wait for me," he responded, grabbing his coat. "I'll give you a ride."

Juice didn't want to leave her company. Being in her presence cleared his mind. Nothing mattered but the present. He didn't think about making money or ruling the world. There was only Brianna and her compelling glow.

He and Brianna slid into the back of his limousine like teenagers on a first date. Brianna got as close to Juice as was physically possible. His anxiety was snatched away by the natural way her head felt on his shoulder, and the sweetness of her fingers in his hand.

When they pulled up in front of her brownstone apartment building on Fifth Avenue, at 125th Street, Brianna insisted that Juice come up for a nightcap.

"You must come up," she said, her eyes flashing as she left the car and headed toward the stoop.

Juice couldn't think of an excuse not to, although the words "small" and "Harlem" came to mind. But that wasn't what made him feel uneasy. He had never been to a female's house. He'd never been invited. He had always done the inviting—mostly to some hotel. But more than that, it was the casualness of Brianna's invitation, as if he were Leroy from down the block. And she wasn't inviting him up in that way. There was an innocence to the invitation, no expectations or preconceived notions.

Brianna wasn't impressed or intimidated that he was Juice Kennedy. She just wanted his company.

Juice instructed Woodrow to drive around.

"I'll text you when I'm ready," he said.

Woodrow knew better than to be a sitting duck in Juice's limo on a Harlem street. He would be close enough, however, so that when the text came, he could be out front before Juice's boot hit the front door.

Juice and Brianna climbed two stories to reach Brianna's apartment. Her place was small, but smartly done up with its high ceilings, tall windows, exposed brick, fireplace, and cutout kitchen. Throughout her apartment, in every room, the walls were decorated with black-and-white photographs or paintings. Juice halted his tour of the apartment in front of a numbered lithograph, Romare Bearden's *Three Women*.

"That's worth a bit," Juice said, pointing at the work.

Brianna didn't hear him, as she'd turned the heat on under a teakettle.

"Juice, I hope you don't mind, but this is all I have to drink, unless you want tap water," she said.

"Should I run out and get something?" Juice offered.

"No. I'm fine if you're fine."

Juice couldn't remember the last time he'd had a cup of tea.

"I'll get the milk," Juice said, opening the refrigerator only to find a head of broccoli, a stick of butter, and a decorative box pushed in the far-right corner.

"No milk, but will you grab that box in there?"

Brianna placed two bright blue mugs on a gray ceramic platter. Juice put the box next to the teapot, and carried the platter to the living room, placing it on the low Asian-style coffee table. Brianna and Juice fit snugly on the red love seat behind the table.

"I know this is a bit close, but the apartment is too small for a full-length sofa," Brianna apologized. "And if your thighs were not so big and strong, I'm sure we would be able to make it work better."

She jokingly slapped Juice on the thigh.

"Ouch!" Juice reacted like an oversize kid.

Brianna poured Juice a cup of tea and handed it to him.

"This isn't Lipton." Juice darted his tongue in and out of his mouth rapidly.

"It is a loose herbal tea, tropical blend. You like?"

"Well, I'm not sure—," Juice began.

"Here," Brianna interrupted. She opened the decorative box. It was full of colorful miniature flowers.

"Take one of these," she said. "Put it on your tongue. Now take a sip of your tea."

"Mmm. It's sweet. I like these candies," said Juice.

"I don't think they're called candy. I have a Japanese friend who doesn't speak much English, so she couldn't explain what these are exactly. She brought them from Japan as a gift and told me to have them with my tea."

Looking around the room, Juice asked, "So, you don't have any money, but you collect art?"

"Is there anything wrong with that?" Brianna said coyly.

"Of course there is," he said. "Don't you think that one day you'll be desperate for money and have to sell one of these images?"

"No way, because on my brokest days, this artwork reminds me that I'm rich in many other ways."

"Do you mind my asking what you're going to do with the advance from the record deal?" Juice questioned.

"My grandmother has Alzheimer's. I'm using the money to pay for the nursing home she's in. She loves to hear me sing, even though she doesn't seem to recognize me anymore. But she always recognizes my singing."

Juice stared into his teacup. Brianna took another one of the candies and guided it toward his mouth. She brushed it across his lips a few times, tickling the outline of his mouth. She finally put the candy in it. She left her finger on his tongue as he closed his mouth around it and gently sucked. She was as sweet as the candy.

"I better go" Juice said, standing up abruptly.

Brianna followed him to the door. "Juice, may I call you Lamar?"

"Yeah, that would be all right." He hadn't allowed anybody to call him James or Lamar since he had earned the name Juice.

He didn't turn around to look at her. He knew that he would

be too tempted to kiss her, and as much as he wanted to do that, and more, he didn't want to ruin this. Juice started down the first flight of stairs, about to text Woodrow to have the car in front. He was halfway down and turned to see, through the banister, Brianna, leaning in the doorway. Her head was tilted to the side and her hair hung slightly over one cheek. Her lips were enticingly parted in a half smile.

Juice's foot wouldn't move another step. He did an about-face and ran back up the stairs, giving Brianna a kiss that stopped time. Brianna leaned her head back and forced her body into Juice's as if she needed his strength to stay on her feet. Her tongue moved around his like a knife being used to layer frosting on a warm cake.

"Don't you think you better get that?" Brianna said, reluctantly pulling away from Juice, feeling the vibration from his pocket.

Juice pulled out his cell phone as Brianna stood on tiptoe to deliver wistful pecks around his neck and jawline.

"Yeah," Juice said, fumbling with his phone. "What? You've got to be kidding! He's in jail?"

Juice didn't sleep, he couldn't sleep. Since Bones had called him with the news of Lil Red's arrest, he'd been pissed. But anger was only fruitful if it bore results and Juice was results oriented. He was thinking and planning. It was now morning and he knocked back the last of his Hennessy. He laid his head back on the couch, trying to relax. He had developed a headache from thinking about Lil Red.

How the fuck did he think he could get on a plane with a gun?

After hearing about the arrest, Juice's first instinct was to have Bones bail him out immediately so Juice could lay into him. But then he thought twice.

"Let his little ass stay in there for a while until I call you," Juice said. "It would be good for him to process the filth and the funk of jail and really get a feel for it. I'll let you know when to spring him."

Lil Red had a posse, but none of them had the money to bail him out. And he wasn't about to call his mother. This wasn't his first offense, and he was on probation. Six months before he'd been caught driving without a license. A couple of months after that, he'd been arrested for assault in Florida.

Three strikes, little motherfucker. Three strikes!

Juice rubbed his temples, thinking about how he would explain the reason Lil Red, nominated for a Grammy for his single, had gotten arrested . . . again. Sure, it gave him street credibility, but that stuff was getting old and tired. The climate was changing and Lil Red was turning out to be more trouble than he was worth. This gun charge was just the tip of the iceberg.

Lil Red, back in his hometown of Jacksonville, Florida, had a beef with the local drug dealer that was only going to get worse. He had been spreading his new money around and moving in on the drug dealer's territory. The guy also didn't like the way Lil Red was walking around as if he was the man.

One of the toughest things for rappers and actors and ballers making that new money is to find out that they can't return to the old neighborhood. They have to use that money to move on because it only breeds jealousy and contempt. It caused Lil Red to walk around wearing a bulletproof vest, like some anorexic 50 Cent, and to buy an arsenal. He'd forgotten to take one of his .38s out of his overnight bag on his way to Richmond for an appearance. This had been the cause of his latest arrest. While too many items get past those baggage-claim people at the airports, a rapper with an entourage will always garner a second look.

Juice knew that the trouble with Lil Red was just starting to brew.

"Make sure you don't get nothing on the couch," Juice growled as he handed the whore a towel. "It's imported cowhide."

The girl giving Juice head was nice looking, no older than twenty, and she was already an old pro.

Juice was getting the best blow job money could buy and he didn't want anything on the plush couch or his clothes. Blow jobs were his mind cleansers. Every time Juice came, it seemed like all the bad things in his head would shoot out of his other head.

He watched as the young woman went to work on his penis with skill, like a snake, practically unhinging her jaw to take it all in, sending rapid charges through his thighs and stomach. He wondered what she could have been if she had chosen to master anything else the way she had mastered sucking dick. And she *was* a master.

Juice busted a nut so fast that he felt like a virgin with no control.

The whore was such an expert that it was only a matter of seconds before Juice was hard again. He fantasized about Brianna as he orgasmed two more times, then he threw a handful of hundreds at the whore and told her to leave.

He went into the bathroom, which was off his study, grabbed a washcloth, and cleaned himself off with warm soapy water. He splashed water on his face and dried it with a hand towel. He then looked in the mirror. He barely recognized himself. Money had a way of changing even the structure of a person's face. It could make a not-so-attractive person as sexy as hell. Juice had started with good stuff, he was already handsome. This face staring back at him was more than handsome; there was something in his eyes that was both alluring and scary. He blinked a couple of times and then shrugged it off. He had work to do; he looked at his watch. He knew Woodrow would be downstairs, on time as always.

Hiring Woodrow full-time was one of the best decisions Juice had made. The driver had proved himself invaluable, loyal, and trustworthy. Juice would see tonight, however, how far he could stretch this man's loyalty. He would be asking Woodrow to do a little more than drive.

When Woodrow drove up, Juice told him to pull into a place where they would switch cars. Juice had a fleet and kept one nondescript car for the times he didn't want to be noticed. This car was equipped with a secret compartment—big enough for a gun—in the back. Juice double-checked to make sure it was still there.

"Woodrow, head down to the Holland Tunnel and get on I-95 South," he told him. "We're going to Richmond, Virginia."

On the ride, he instructed Bones to have Lil Red bailed out in exactly six hours. Juice calculated that they would get to Richmond in five and a half hours. They arrived at the Richmond Detention Center on Ninth Street right on time. He had gotten a text message from Bones that Lil Red should be getting out shortly, that the bail had been taken care of. Juice instructed Woodrow to drive around the block once so he could see all the exits. It would take a little time for Lil Red to be processed. There was a perfect route, leading right back to I-95.

Like clockwork, Lil Red came bopping out of the detention center carrying the brown paper bag with his belongings in it. He put his big diamond-encrusted watch back on his skinny wrist. He counted the hundreds, then neatly folded them and put them in his back pocket. He then took out his cell to call one of his boys who lived nearby to pick him up. Before he got off the steps, Juice instructed Woodrow to pull up. Juice rolled down the back passenger-side window, which was closest to the sidewalk where Lil Red was standing. He rolled it down just enough to be able to put the nose of his .45, with a silencer, out the window. He squeezed off five shots—three hit the center of Lil Red's chest, one hit him in the thigh, and the other one lodged in the right temple.

Woodrow didn't see that coming and almost started panicking, but Juice's calm voice stopped him.

"I need you to drive like normal and head to I-95," Juice said.

Woodrow gripped the wheel to keep his hands from shaking. *Is this motherfucker crazy or what? I didn't sign up for this!*

But he drove as if a man hadn't just gotten gunned down on a city street. Juice knew from growing up on the mean streets of Newark that the best place to kill someone was close to a jail or a police station. He wasn't worried about anyone chasing them. Woodrow didn't begin to really calm down until he hit Perryville, which told him he was close to the New Jersey Turnpike. His heart had been beating so fast he could almost hear it over the music that Juice asked him to play. Woodrow got them back to New York by two in the morning. He was exhausted, more exhausted than he had ever been. And he was emotionally drained.

Woodrow had done a lot of things in his life, and a lot of the things he wasn't proud of. But he had never witnessed a killing or been part of one. He was now officially an accomplice to murder, a fact Juice reminded him of shortly after he pulled up in front of Juice's place.

"Woodrow, I really appreciate your loyalty," Juice said. "And your involvement tonight will be handsomely rewarded. I'm going to take care of you; you know that. I know I can trust you not to say a word to anyone—not a soul. Do I have your word?"

Woodrow didn't know what to say except yes. He now knew what this man was capable of.

"That's very good," Juice said. "Check out your bank account tomorrow afternoon. I think you will be very pleased. You can have the next two days off. I figure you'll want to go on a shopping spree. But get ready, because we will have a lot to do next week."

Woodrow sat outside Juice's place for about thirty minutes before driving home. He thought he was in a bad dream and kept squeezing his eyes shut, then opening them, hoping that the image of that young boy sprawled on a Virginia street with blood everywhere would just go away. But it wouldn't.

At the Jacksonville Memorial Gardens, fans of Timothy "Lil Red" Reddington showed up in large numbers. His underground hits and his single had afforded him a great deal of attention, as well as paving the way for his much-anticipated CD, which was scheduled for release the next month. The pallbearers—consisting of a couple of his posse, his brother, and his cousins—surrounded the white hearse. All the men were dressed in black suits. There was a sea of black suits, except for Juice, who showed up in a cream-colored Armani. He loved how Armani looked on him and this was a spectacle where he would be seen, so he needed to look good.

The only other people to stand out were two white men in tan trench coats. It was whispered at the funeral that they were detectives from New York.

Juice pretended not to notice them.

The minister stepped up to the makeshift podium at the grave site. He looked like a cross between James Brown and Prince—in the Little Richard vein. Taking out a piece of paper he said, "I would like to share with you some final words. The Reddington family would like to thank you all for your love and support, and for offering your comfort and companionship during their time of grief. Timothy's life is a great loss for all of us. I would like to share a reading of "In the Event of My Demise," from Timothy's favorite rapper, Mr. Tupac Shakur.

While the minister recited the poem Juice leaned over to Bones and whispered, "That cat wasn't no Tupac."

Under normal circumstances, Bones would have gotten a chuckle out of that. But he'd really liked Lil Red and wasn't feeling Juice's callousness.

On Juice's other side was Brianna Banks, whose newly released CD had debuted at number one just days before. She was wearing a tasteful fitted black suit. She wanted to support her labelmate; Lil Red had contributed a rhyme to the remix of Brianna's next single. And she had gotten to really know him that day in the studio. He was so playful and charming.

"Boy, you better get away from me before I put you in my purse and take you home with me," Brianna had said to him teasingly. "You are so cute."

"Oh, please," he'd said. "Please, please, please take me home with you!"

Brianna was thinking about the last laughs the two had shared as they began to lower his coffin into the ground. She got choked up, and Juice broke down, visibly weeping. Brianna rubbed his back as he crouched on the ground, crying.

On the plane back to New York, Juice, Brianna, and Bones sat in somber silence, Brianna dabbing at her eyes with a tissue.

"So young, so young," she said.

"I know," Juice chimed in. "Lil Red's death has been really hard for me to take. You know, all I ever wanted was to see my people succeed beyond even their wildest dreams. Where I come from, I'm not supposed to even be here. I had to raise myself, so all I've ever tried to do is provide opportunities for these kids. I just wanted to show them a better life. To see him go out like this hurts."

Brianna listened intently, hanging on Juice's every word. She was fascinated by this complicated man. Bones turned toward the window, rolling his eyes.

"I may seem tough, but it's only out of defense," Juice said, turning on his fake emotion. "You can't imagine the things I've had to deal with on a daily basis."

"No, I can't imagine," she said.

"Hey, I just had an idea," Juice said. "Would you participate in a tribute album for Lil Red? I would really like to raise some money for his moms. I know he talked about buying her a house in a nice neighborhood."

"I would be honored."

A few weeks after his brutal killing, Lil Red was immortal-ized. Juice had not only released a tribute album in re-cord time, but he'd also released Lil Red's debut CD. They both became instant hits. The tribute CD, featuring Brianna Banks, went triple platinum in just three weeks.

"That nigga is worth way more to me dead," said Juice to Bones, while reading the trade papers in his office. "I mean, can you believe these numbers? Yo, I haven't seen this kind of profit in years. Like I said, that little fucker is worth more to me dead."

Bones was surprised by the callousness. Instead of mourning such a lost soul, he couldn't believe that Juice was salivating over potential profit. The truth behind Lil Red's death was yet an-other secret Juice had been keeping. Juice had finally let Bones in on some of the Seven Figures dealing. But that was out of necessity. He needed Bones to take care of some of their business. So he had to know some of what was going on—but not all of it.

"Shit, if I had known this would happen . . ." Juice didn't finish his statement.

"What? Finish that," Bones said.

Juice was silent, pretending not to hear Bones.

"So what really happened that night Lil Red was arrested?" Bones asked. "It's bugging the fuck out of me. I get him sprung and within ten minutes he's gunned down. How the fuck did that happen?"

Bones was staring at Juice, looking for breaks in his body language or something else that would give him a clue. But Juice was completely unreadable.

"I don't know," Juice said. "I guess he pissed off the wrong motherfucker. You know he had a few enemies. But don't go getting all soft on me. Whoever killed that little fucker did us a favor. Wait until you see your bonus check."

"You're a cold motherfucker," was all Bones could say.

"No, get it straight, I'm a *rich* motherfucker," Juice responded.

"You're just a motherfucker," Bones said, leaving the room.

Bones had an uneasy feeling about the shooting of Lil Red. He couldn't shake it. He knew that whatever had happened would eventually come out. He was a patient man; he would wait.

Since the basketball game a few weeks before, Audrey had been on cloud nine. Rather than focusing all her attention on work, she spent her time daydreaming about her romantic possibilities with Xavier and Bones. An embarrassment of riches. Two men, both seemingly well off, both very handsome and both very different.

"This must have been how that chick felt in Spike Lee's *She's Gotta Have It,*" Audrey said aloud to no one in particular.

On one side she had Bones, who, while she hadn't had a chance to spend any real time with him, pushed her buttons in ways no other man had. He was serious, quiet, and strong. He would never let her get away with her BS and she liked that about him. He was a man's man and he made her feel safe.

Xavier was more refined, more the kind of man you could

travel with to exotic places. Where she could see herself teaching something to Bones, with Xavier, Audrey could be the student. He was self-made, too, which she loved.

Both men were very different from the bums Audrey usually attracted, the kind she settled for out of desperation. She was glad she'd taken that long hiatus from dating. It had given her time to appreciate all that she had to offer and realize what she deserved in turn. And she felt that God was rewarding her for being faithful.

While both were still enigmas to Audrey, she convinced herself that she would be proud to have either man at her side.

Xavier had an edge simply in the time he'd spent with Audrey. The two shared several intimate lunches and dinners, whereas her interactions with Bones had been through telephone conversations. She placed no demands and had no expectations with either of these men. Instead she was patiently allowing their relationships to evolve naturally—a new approach for a woman who enjoyed being in control. She'd decided a new approach to her love life was in order.

Audrey was surprised when Bones called her on a Tuesday morning. He had never called her during the workday, saying he had respect for her job and never wanted to be a distraction. The truth was, he was too busy in class or studying or doing Juice's bidding during the day to call her. Bones normally called in the late evening.

"Dinner is tonight at seven. I know you're going to be looking good," Bones said.

"Presumptuous, aren't you," she said. "Maybe I have plans for tonight."

"Seven o'clock okay?" Bones said. "And all beautiful women have plans, but they cancel them when they want to."

She did have plans. And she was going to cancel them.

Audrey had the rest of the day to think about what she would wear. She sat at her desk beaming like some sixteen-year-old anticipating prom night. Audrey hit the speaker button on her office phone to check her messages. There was a message from the head of the company:

"Hi, Audrey. We need a representative from the parent company at our new branch in Vegas. We need you to go out there and set things up for us. Please call me and let me know your schedule. I'm out of the office until Friday, but you can call me on my cell. I need you there. Okay. Let me know. Thanks."

Audrey turned on her computer and began to answer her email. The second in her in-box was from the new manager of the Atlanta branch. He was looking forward to meeting with her in Vegas and wanted to know if she would arrive Thursday or Friday.

By the time Audrey finished answering her email, signing, and copying documents, it was already one o'clock in the afternoon. She decided she would fly out Thursday afternoon, giving her Wednesday to run errands and try to slip in a hair appointment.

Audrey's office phone rang and the caller ID let her know it was Linda.

"Hey, girl," said Audrey, biting her bottom lip.

"Don't even try it!" Linda said. "You were supposed to call me weeks ago with details. All I get is, 'I got in safely.' What was that? Tell me about this Bones character. Don't even waste your time apologizing, just tell me what's going on with you!"

"Okay, I'm sorry," Audrey said, apologizing anyway. "For the record, I've been *very* busy at work. I haven't gone out with

Bones yet, but we have a date tonight. I feel wicked because I'm canceling my date with Xavier to go out with Bones."

"Xavier?" Linda said. "Okay, sneaky Petey. Who's Xavier? I let you out one night and you go buck wild!"

"Well, Xavier and I met at the game, too," Audrey explained. "Actually, we reconnected. He went to Pitt with us. You probably don't remember him because you were too busy actually going to school and being a mom to enjoy those extracurricular activities. But he was one of the stars on the team. Might have made it to the NBA if he hadn't torn up his knee. But he seems to have done okay for himself despite that."

"So you're canceling a date with him to go out with Bones?" Linda was confused.

"Yes," Audrey said. "I don't know what it is about Bones, but I'm really attracted to him."

"And you're not so attracted to this other guy?" Linda asked.

"I am, but it's just different," she said. "I can't explain it. I wish I could mush them together and make one man."

"Girl, you are a mess!" Linda said. "You better pick one and be happy and stop playing games. Juggling men makes you no better than a man who has a chick on the side. It's just not right."

"Okay, Miss Perfect," Audrey said. "Not everyone can be as fortunate, having Captain America live with them. Mr. Everything. Just count your blessings and let me figure this out."

"Just be careful, sweetie," Linda said, getting serious. "I want you to be happy, but be careful."

"I will," Audrey said. "I'm going out with Bones tonight, then on Thursday I leave for Las Vegas for work. Don't panic if you don't hear from me for a few days. Okay?"

"Hey, you know, Carl said something about going to Vegas on

business. I'll have to check when. Maybe you two might be there
at the same time and could hook up or something."

"Like that could happen, girl," Audrey joked. "You know your
man is *all* business. If he's there for business, he won't have any
time to babysit me."

"Okay," Linda said. "You're right. But keep me posted."

Audrey hung up, then picked up the receiver again and dialed Xavier.

"Hello, this is Audrey Williams calling for Xavier Prince . . .
Hi, sweetie, did I catch you at a bad time? . . . Unfortunately, I
have to go away on business and am unable to keep our date for
tonight . . . Las Vegas . . . No way! . . . When do you leave? . . .
We'll just have to go out there . . . I look forward . . . Call me on
my cell when you arrive."

In the summer months, Manhattan was an amazing, electrify-
ing city. The sidewalks on the Upper West Side were full of
proud, expressionless West Indian nannies pushing carriages
holding white babies; young women and men suited up in running gear or carrying tennis racquets and heading for Central
Park to exercise; and stylishly dressed professionals strutting in
expensive, well-made suits and lugging imported totes. These
people moved around the neighborhood effortlessly, careful not
to make eye contact with anyone. Audrey and Bones met at the
Shark Bar on Manhattan's Upper West Side.

The restaurant/bar had been around for a number of years and
was recognized as a meeting ground for primarily upscale black
people, artistic types, and on occasion a sprinkling of celebrities
such as rapper LL Cool J and actor Ruben Santiago. Its Southern-
style food was moderately priced. The restaurant's decor was

simple, with exposed brick in the bar area and rich velvet curtains encasing the booths in the dining room to allow for privacy.

Audrey and Bones were there early enough to enjoy the privacy of a booth, and to avoid having to struggle through the normally crowded bar area.

"I know we only met a couple of weeks ago, and I don't know you that well, but you look a bit different than I remember," Audrey stated with sincerity.

"I don't know what you mean," Bones said, smiling.

"That's what was missing—your smile," Audrey exclaimed, smiling back.

"Yeah, actually, lately I'm only smiling when I'm talking to you," Bones confessed.

"You aren't gassing me up, are you?"

"Nah, just been working hard learning the club business. And I had to go to a funeral the other day, Lil Red."

"It was on the news!" said Audrey. "I didn't know you were close to him."

"He was on my cousin's record label," Bones said. "I got to know the little dude. He was very funny and had a bright future."

"Yeah," was all Audrey could say. "That's crazy."

"His death has me thinking," he said. "I've been thinking that it's important who you hang with. I know that's no huge revelation. But you must live every moment doing things that you are proud of. If you do something you are not proud of, someone has something to hold over you. If someone has something to hold over you, then you are never free."

Completely missing the point, Audrey responded, "Yes, Lil Red is free."

"What you been doing to keep busy besides keeping yourself fine?" Bones said, grinning again.

"Work, work, and more work." Audrey failed to mention Xavier. "In fact, I'm glad that we're seeing each other tonight. I'll be leaving for Vegas in a couple of days and staying until Monday afternoon."

"Why do you sound so annoyed? It's Vegas. It doesn't get much better than that."

"Yeah, but it's business," said Audrey. "It's not like I'm going to be around a bunch of people I want to hang out with."

"It's Vegas. You don't need anybody to have fun there," he said.

"Bones, you can certainly take my place if you'd like."

"Well, I can do you one better. How about if I meet you out there and show you just how good a time Vegas can be?"

"Are you serious?" said Audrey, a surprised expression on her face.

"This date was about seeing if you could come with *me* to Vegas," he said. "That, and the fact that I wanted to see you again. I've got club-related business out there this weekend."

"I don't believe you!" Audrey replied. "What is this? Fate or something? I mean, really? You are going to be in *Vegas* for the weekend?"

"Yep," he said. "I guess it is kind of weird. But I believe that things happen for a reason."

Audrey was beginning to think that the stars were lining up for her. What were the odds that this man—*and Xavier!*—would be in Vegas at the exact same time she would be?

If Bones was lying and was just going to show up to be with her, she loved that, too, because it meant that he had money and could afford to just hop on a plane with no advance notice. While Audrey didn't consider herself a gold digger, she believed a man with means was just easier to love.

Las Vegas, Nevada, or specifically, a stretch of land in the middle of the desert, labeled "the strip," was the best location in the world for hiding dirty laundry. Since so many wild acts were committed there, nothing was viewed as being suspect. It was the kind of crazy town where couples could get married by an Elvis look-alike; where Wayne Newton had become one of the most successful entertainers of all time; and where two men with tigers ruled—until one tiger lost his mind and mauled one of them. There were so many distractions in this desert that most people could slip in and out unnoticed.

It was the perfect place for the next Seven Figures meeting. It also helped that a few of the members needed to be there for a special announcement. Carl had rallied his connections in the financial arena, along with Langston, the head of the corporate legal division at Renard's firm, to hammer out a deal with the National Basketball Association. They sweet-talked and double-talked the NBA commissioner until the organization conceded that Xavier would be the primary owner of the Vegas Vipers, a new franchise. There would be a weekend of press conferences and celebrations.

Xavier was the first member to have his dream materialize. In these three days, the members would also celebrate teamwork.

As for Bones, he was finding out that there would be much more work than play. Juice had him on a tight schedule, fulfilling near-impossible, last-minute, and insane requests. Instructed by Juice, Bones was responsible for ensuring that the men of the Seven Figures were thoroughly entertained, in whatever fashion each man desired.

To launch this weekend of debauchery, in one of the suites at the Bellagio, Bones had created the "Den of Anything Goes." Here, the members would live out their wildest fantasies. In addition to the suite, Bones had rented out the penthouse. Complete with ornate, over-the-top Roman-style decor, it spanned seven floors and required a key for access. To guide Bones, Juice had given his friend a list of items the businessmen would require in order to fulfill their desires, ranging from exotic foods to unusual sex toys. LaJuan's name was on the list. Bones thought about questioning Juice about this, but instead just made the arrangements for LaJuan's overnight stay to avoid unnecessary drama. However, the request made Bones more intrigued about Juice's secret club.

When Bones arrived at the airport, he was disappointed to see that LaJuan had brought along his roommate,

Jacob. Bones knew that LaJuan was book smart, but he couldn't believe how little common sense the former student had.

"He can't stay here," Bones said without greeting the boys.

"What do you mean? I'm paying for him, plus he has his own credit cards," protested LaJuan.

"It ain't about the money. He just doesn't belong here. LaJuan, you don't bring your friends to the job," Bones explained.

"I just thought I could introduce him to some of my friends, that's all."

"These men are *not* your friends," warned Bones. "This was a dumb move, a very dumb move!"

It was too late to send him back, but Bones didn't like it. He was paid handsomely for taking care of his cousin's business, and he did so as professionally as possible. In this vein, he phoned Juice to let him know that LaJuan had a friend with him.

"Whatever happens in Vegas stays in Vegas . . . right?" Juice said, already in party mode.

When Audrey arrived, Las Vegas hit her right in the face as soon as she deboarded the airplane. It was sensory overload; lights were flashing and she heard the *ding, ding, ding,* of the one-armed bandits. Even the airport lobby looked like a casino. There were droves of people gambling everywhere. When she escaped outside, she was immediately met by the desert heat. She'd been outside for only the few minutes it took to catch a cab and her hair was starting to fall. She needed to get to the air-conditioned environment of the Luxor Hotel quickly. Her freshly done hair would never stand up under the pressure of the Vegas heat.

She had never been to Vegas before, and it wasn't on her wish list. Travel commercials about the town made the place seem plastic and out of control. But on the drive down the strip,

Audrey came to appreciate Vegas's magic. It was similar to Times Square, with all its bright lights and flashing billboards, but multiplied by ten. The strip consisted of a three- to four-mile long stretch of interconnected theme hotels. There was the Luxor, which embraced an Egyptian theme and was constructed as a gigantic pyramid, which could be seen from an airplane flying over Las Vegas. There was the Venetian, with gondolas that allowed its guests to travel by water from one location to another. Caesar's Palace displayed huge statues of Roman gods and had planetarium-like light shows. There was the Paris, a hotel featuring the Eiffel Tower as its centerpiece, with dancing cancan girls circling the lobby. These lavish hotels, thoroughly equipped with roulette tables, slot machines, poker tables, and other places to gamble, were larger than life.

Audrey was minutes from her hotel when her phone began to vibrate. It was a text message from Xavier.

> Whatcha doing? I'm at the
> Bellagio. You want some
> company?

Audrey checked into her hotel. She unpacked and freshened up, trying to do something with her hair. While she'd hoped that Bones would call first, she had agreed to meet Xavier in the lobby.

Hey, stranger," she said, leaning in to give Xavier a kiss on the cheek. "So what's planned?"

"I don't believe in plans," Xavier said. "I just wanted to see you. I turned my phone off for the evening. So let's go for a walk."

On the strip, since all the hotels and casinos were linked, they didn't have to walk outside into the desert heat. They strolled to the Bellagio, which was said to have a botanical garden that was breathtaking. Xavier reached over and took Audrey's hand. She squeezed his hand lightly and Xavier smiled.

"What kind of business are you doing here?" Audrey asked.

"On Sunday, the NBA will be making the announcement that I will be the owner of my own franchise."

Audrey started screaming and jumping up and down as if she had won a jackpot. She was with a man who owned a basketball team—this was all that ran through her mind. She could see herself sitting courtside at every game, reminiscent of her college years. Xavier appreciated her enthusiasm.

"I am now about to live out my wildest dreams. I am so blessed," continued Xavier.

"Yes, very blessed," said Audrey, as she did the monetary calculations in her head.

When they arrived at the garden, the divine smell was the first thing that hit Audrey. It was a sweet, fresh, exotic floral essence that wafted around the entrance. Audrey and Xavier walked hand in hand toward the gazebo, which was surrounded by water and white and yellow water lilies. Audrey imagined a wedding there, complete with tall basketball-playing groomsmen. After spending some time gazing into each other's eyes they floated over to the gondolas, where they sat together in a small boat and toured the hotel by water. They were served champagne while being serenaded by opera singers.

"Will you please come up to my room for a nightcap?" Xavier asked.

"Lead the way," Audrey said.

Each Seven Figures member had arrived and checked into the Bellagio Hotel under an assumed name for this weekend of adventure. Upon their arrival, there was a short meeting to update each guest on the status of his professional goals. The group was excited by the swiftness of Xavier's attaining an NBA team. It served as proof to the men that Juice was serious, and that within the group they had the power to accomplish anything when they pooled their resources and influence.

The NBA brass were strong-armed by Carl and by Renard's firm to take a chance on Xavier. They weren't willing, however, to allow Xavier to buy an established team, but they had been considering a franchise in Vegas for some time, even before they'd held their NBA all-star game in Sin City a couple of years before. New Orleans was another option, but the Seven Figures pushed for Vegas.

Juice made the announcement that Xavier Prince would be the proud owner of the Vegas Vipers. The deal included their having the number one pick for the next draft. Hearing this announcement was a big release for Xavier. A dream he had had for many years was finally coming to fruition. He felt empowered by the accomplishment, as well as overwhelmed by emotion.

"Thank you so much, brothers, for your support," Xavier said. "You cannot imagine the great sense of satisfaction I feel. I want you all to share my elation, and I will work with all of you to ensure that your dreams are realized as well. This achievement is not about my individual gain, it is about empowering an entire race. I will use my new position to show others that we have the knowledge, talent, and resources to accomplish anything we desire."

After the applause, Juice took the floor again.

"This is just beginning—for all of you," he reminded them. "Senator Hernandez, I have some good news for you as well, which I will share with you later."

Juice looked around the room. He saw the eager eyes of the men, all on him, all longing, all expectation. They believed in Juice and the vote of confidence made him full of himself. Juice was drunk with power. He'd always imagined having it all. Now he actually *did* have it all—more money than he knew what to do with, all the sex he could desire, and influence over people's destiny.

"Gentlemen, the weekend is just beginning," Juice announced. "There are robes in the other room and a black mask for each of you. We must protect our identities. Keep in mind that everyone has been completely checked out—right down to medical clearances. You are also welcome to just watch if you want. Come on, I don't want to miss out on one minute of fun!"

The members took the private elevator down three floors. They were astounded when the doors opened. The spacious area looked like something out of a wild carnival. Bones had done an amazing job in getting the place set up for the men. Xavier couldn't believe his eyes and ears. Music was pumping, filling the room with primitive African rhythms. The lights were dim, complemented by perfectly situated candles. Along the perimeter there were semicircle dividers where men or women were gyrating, wearing only gold wreaths on their heads. Masked waiters were carrying trays holding liquor, marijuana, and cocaine.

The men were eager to get their party on. Juice stripped his clothing off and approached one of the dividers, closing the curtain behind him. A couple of the other men removed their clothing and either went to the bar or behind one of the curtains. Xavier was the last person left standing in the entranceway. This was not his scene. Once his eyes adjusted to the darkness, he noticed, in one corner of the room, a young man who looked equally uncomfortable. He made a beeline for him.

"So do you come here often?" said Xavier, trying to comprehend what was happening around him. "Don't worry. I don't get down like this. You just look like you weren't with this either."

"I'm Jacob. This is my first time. And you're right, I'm not feeling this at all. I thought a few drinks might loosen things up for me, but it's only given me a headache."

"I think I have some aspirin in my room," Xavier offered.

Jacob looked at him sideways.

"Seriously, I'm not propositioning you."

Jacob didn't move. Surprised by the nature of LaJuan's hustle, Jacob wasn't sure who he could trust anymore. He scanned the room, then did a double take. There was a masked man acting wild, grabbing two younger men. He playfully chased them into one of the cubicles.

"Yo, these dudes don't waste any time," Jacob said.

"Excuse me?" Xavier replied, confused.

"Nothing," Jacob said, as there was something familiar about the chasing man, something that forced Jacob to approach the curtained cubicle for a better look. The chaser was bent over, allowing one younger man to mount him while the other young man was kneeling in front of him, servicing him.

"Oh my God!" Jacob said loudly, but his words couldn't be heard above the music. He saw a familiar fraternity brand on the left thigh of the man being pleasured. Jacob blinked hard a few times to make sure he was seeing what he thought he was. Unmistakably, it was Carl.

"Where did you say your room was?" Jacob returned to Xavier's side. "I really need that aspirin."

Before they were able to reach the door, Jacob threw up violently.

After a night of wild, crazy, fun-filled play, the members of the Seven Figures were eager to complete their business. It was time to go public with Xavier's acquisition. The press conference was held at the foot of the Eiffel Tower at the Paris Las Vegas, a crowd of several hundred in attendance. At the front of the group were representatives from the National Basketball Association. They looked official and dignified in their dark blue suits. The flashing lights from the cameras were competing with the best light shows in Vegas when the NBA commissioner took the podium. He gave a humorous congratulatory speech that caused the crowd to erupt, then he welcomed Xavier, turning the press conference over to him.

"This is a wonderful opportunity for the sport of basketball, just as it is for me personally," Xavier began. "With my European connections, I plan to be an asset for the NBA in its overseas expansion. And in my new capacity, I plan to bring the city of Vegas even more excitement—if that's possible . . ."

Somewhere at the back of the crowd were Audrey and Bones, basking in the comfort of each other's presence. Audrey, though, couldn't seem to keep her eyes off Xavier. She was beaming as he spoke at the podium.

"Do you know old boy?" asked Bones.

"What are you talking about?"

"I don't know, but ever since he took the podium you have been all like this." Bones started rapidly batting his eyelashes while dancing on his tiptoes and clapping his hands together using only his fingertips.

"I have *not* been doing that," responded Audrey, not amused.

"Well, girl, that's how you're acting. You know this cat or something?"

"I met him the same night I met you," she said.

"I'm not sharing you," said Bones confidently.

"Bones, Xavier and I have gone out a few times, whereas you seem too busy for me," Audrey confessed. "Look, I've been here in Vegas the whole weekend and this is the first time we've seen each other, and this wasn't even planned."

"Yeah, you're right," he conceded. "This weekend was tougher than I'd imagined. I had more work to do than I thought, but I called you several times and you were in meetings."

"I need a man who is available," she said. "I haven't been to your house, or anything. For all I know, you could be married."

"Now, you know I'm not married," Bones said, slightly hurt. "My job has placed a lot of demands on my time lately. I'm sure you can relate to that. There's no reason to imagine the worst.

Once we are back in the city, I promise to spend more time with you."

"Well, we'll see what happens," she said, folding her arms and watching Xavier getting pats on the back after his speech.

"Don't act like you don't feel what I feel when we're together," he said.

Audrey looked at Bones and there was that smile and she melted.

"Yeah, I do," Audrey said, smiling, temporarily forgetting about Xavier and his basketball team.

"So stop playing," Bones said, leaning in to kiss her.

Juice got off the plane feeling great. The Vegas trip had been a hit, and he was riding high. One of Juice's cell phones came to life. Bones looked at the number and tossed the phone to Juice. He knew that Juice would want to answer this one himself.

"Hello, Miss Banks," Juice said. "I'm glad you called. I didn't expect to hear from you."

"You *had* to expect to hear something after those flowers you sent!" said Brianna.

"Oh, you got those? Well, it was only a little something to let you know that just because I haven't been in the studio with you, I'm thinking about you."

"I'm on my way to a spa appointment now. But I'm going to be doing some work at the studio tonight. I would love your input."

"Of course. That sounds like a real nice night to me," Juice said.

After receiving the remainder of the advance money for her album, and the payment for her contribution on Lil Red's tribute album, Brianna moved into a huge house in Fort Lee, New Jersey. It had a massive front lawn that was tastefully landscaped. The house rested on top of a small hill. There were traces of light coming from other houses that were at least a quarter of a mile away.

She's done good things with her money. I like that, Juice said to himself as he walked up to the door and rang the bell.

One of the men working with Brianna let Juice in. He led him through the huge gourmet kitchen with its bleached white-wood floors, and white marble island with copper pots hanging above it. The two took a left off the kitchen and went down a spiral staircase that led to the studio Brianna had had built.

It rivaled the old Hit Factory in Manhattan, with its high-gloss wooden floor and top-of-the-line equipment. At the bottom of the stairs was a nice-size sitting area complete with a fifty-inch plasma TV. EA Sports blared across the screen. Juice located Brianna in the soundproof booth. She was moving her head to the beat. As soon as she saw Juice, she gestured for him to come in.

She got up from the leather seat facing the boards.

"Hey, I'm so happy that you made it," she exclaimed, reaching around for a hug. "Let me introduce you to everyone."

"Please, Brianna," said one of the engineers. "We *all* know Juice Kennedy!"

Brianna and Juice started cracking up. "I like this beat right here," Juice said, blasting what he knew would be a hit. "That's sweet!" He was itching to take control of the boards, to take the beat to an even higher place. It had been a few months since he'd been in the studio with Brianna.

The house intercom buzzed and the room cleared out faster than a school at three o'clock. The food Brianna had ordered earlier arrived. Juice found himself alone with her.

"I love seeing you in your element," said Juice. "But I don't know if I can handle you being around all these men."

"Well, if *you* were my man, you wouldn't have a thing to worry about, now would you?" responded Brianna as she grabbed his hand, pulling his chair closer to her.

Juice couldn't believe his nervousness. *What is it about her?* He had been onstage at Madison Square Garden before thirty-thousand-plus screaming fans and it didn't compare with the level of excitement he felt in Brianna's presence. He had been on national television before millions, had traveled the world, and had never been this anxious.

Brianna smiled. "I decided to add another song I wrote to the album," she said. "I want you to hear this. I want your opinion."

Brianna went to work on the boards like a real pro, cueing up the song and checking the levels so that Juice could hear it pitch perfect. He was surprised that she could work the boards.

Juice tried to listen, but the truth was that he couldn't concentrate. The more she focused and played with the buttons, the more turned on he got. She was beautiful, smart, and talented, too. He put his hand on her waist. Her body was hard in the right places and soft in the best places. Juice could hardly contain himself.

"You know, I have some music I would love you to hear if you don't mind," Juice said, interrupting Brianna's playing of her song.

"Of course I don't mind," she responded.

She waited for him to pull out a CD or a thumb drive.

"You need to get your coat."

"Oh, you mean you want me to hear something somewhere else?" she asked. "You mean right *now?*"

"Yeah, right now," Juice said, grabbing her hand and heading for the stairs.

Once in the car, Brianna eased back into the comfortable Phantom Rolls-Royce. The leather seat felt like an expensive living room couch. She could sleep right there. The ride was smooth, more like a balanced, powerful jet than a car. Brianna and Juice talked nonstop until they were interrupted by Woodrow, letting them know they had reached Juice's brownstone on the Upper East Side of Manhattan. Engrossed in the conversation, Brianna hadn't realized they had crossed the George Washington Bridge. It was less than a twenty-minute ride from Fort Lee, but it was a world away.

"Okay, when I open the door, we're going to run up the steps," Juice said to Brianna. "I don't want anyone to see us."

Juice was holding something in his hand.

"What's that?" Brianna asked.

"This is the remote control to my front door," he replied. "And it controls just about everything in my house. You ready?"

Juice hit the button, causing the lights to come on in the hallway, just behind the two large wooden doors with oval glass insets covered with white curtains. He grabbed her hand and tapped on the glass, signaling to Woodrow to open the car door. The two jumped out and ran up the brownstone steps.

Inside, Juice took Brianna straight to the studio. He immediately started hitting buttons, bringing the studio to life.

"Listen to this," he said. "It's something I've been working on in my spare time."

"Like you have spare time," Brianna snickered.

"Yeah, I know," he said, chuckling. "I know if you sing this song, it'll cause the next baby boom for sure."

Brianna loved the seductive opening chords. She closed her eyes and started to feel the music.

"I think the woman singing sounds great," she said, humming the chorus.

"Yeah, she's good," Juice replied. "But if you sing it, it would be like Maxwell singing Robin Thicke's 'Lost Without You.' You know he would have taken that song to a whole other level."

Brianna knew instantly what Juice was saying. Maxwell would have ripped up that song, definitely taking it to another level. Brianna was feeling Juice's tune. She wanted to see if she could be that Maxwell to this woman's Robin Thicke.

"Let's do it," said Brianna.

She took off her jacket and began listening more intently to the music, trying to memorize words and keys and pitches.

Juice escorted her into the booth on the other side of the glass. Brianna slid the headphones on and made herself comfortable on the black stool, positioned in front of the microphone.

"Okay, Brianna. We're going to take it from the top." Juice couldn't help but stare at Brianna. He was as mesmerized now as he'd been the very first night he'd heard her sing.

Brianna sang the words to his song, "If I Love You, Will You Love Me Back?" She belted out those words, feeling every one of them, looking straight at Juice, who returned the stare. Their eyes were locked for what seemed like an eternity. Juice swallowed hard, feeling his penis start to rise. He got up from his chair, his eyes still locked on Brianna, like a hunter on its prey. He entered the booth, and he and Brianna were face-to-face. Juice pulled her to him and kissed her with all his might.

Brianna moved away for a second, to hit a switch on the control panel. Suddenly the room was filled with her voice singing the song that made them both hot. She turned it up, loud. She backed away from him, slowly removing her clothes. He stared at her body. Her skin looked like milk-chocolate silk; her nipples were erect; her hair was cascading around her shoulders.

Juice moved toward her. He lifted his shirt over his head, not bothering to unbutton it. He unbuckled his belt and let his pants fall to his ankles. He stepped out of his pants and pulled down his boxers. Brianna let out a gasp and they both smiled. He guided her to him and kissed her again. It was a hungry kiss as their tongues battled for space. His penis was pressing against her with an urgency that made her back up; he lifted her without effort onto the leather stool.

When he lifted her up, her breasts were in his face. He started sucking them—going from one nipple to the other, back and forth, slowly, as if he was eating a chocolate-covered strawberry with all of the liquid dripping down his chin.

Brianna moaned. Her moan, coupled with her voice flowing through the speakers, drove Juice wild. He sucked harder. Brianna grabbed the back of his head and directed him to her hot spot. He licked and sucked his way down toward her pussy. Juice stopped and looked up; Brianna's head was thrown back and her eyes were closed in anticipation.

Juice dove in, tongue first, then, putting two fingers inside the warm, wet pussy, he sucked lightly on her clitoris with his long, thick tongue. He moved his tongue gently back and forth across her love button. Brianna pushed her hips toward Juice's mouth. He applied more pressure to her clit with his tongue, while moving his fingers in and out of her pussy and sneaking his lubricated thumb into her anus. Brianna screamed in delight as she came, her pussy on fire.

Completely turned on, Juice rubbed his dick to relieve some of the pressure. He wanted to make her come again and again. He continued to manipulate her body until she came again. He then stood up in front of her, chest heaving, trying to catch his breath. Brianna got down on her knees, weak from what this man had just done to her. Juice glided into her pussy from behind. Her canal was pulsating and she could barely hold herself up. Juice reached around and rubbed her clit while not missing a stroke. Brianna was panting and moaning. Her inner walls began to grip and tug at his penis, which was a very snug fit. Her delicious pussy made him lose control. Juice pumped faster and harder, loving her hot wetness, which tightly enveloped him.

Brianna pulled away and turned on her back. She wanted to feel all that he had to give her and she wanted to look into his face. Juice eagerly reentered her warmth. She drew him deeper inside by raising her hips off the floor, bucking against him. She met Juice stroke for stroke, digging her fingernails into his ass, until neither one of them was able to control their release. She slid one of her hands off his butt and stroked his balls. The sensation sent chills up Juice's spine as the two of them came together.

Brianna was spent and so was he. Juice scooped her up and held her in his lap, wrapping his well-defined arms around her. He felt no pain or guilt, only complete satisfaction and contentment.

There was an awkward silence in Jacob and LaJuan's apartment. Immersed in his thoughts, Jacob had not had much to say to his roommate since they'd returned from Vegas. Jacob opened his backpack, which he had not touched for a couple of weeks. He checked his schedule and decided there was no time like the present to get back to the familiar academic grind. He was ready to make up for the time he had missed chasing the fast life.

Jacob grabbed his bag and car keys. He drove the ten blocks to campus deep in thought. Last year he had made the dean's list. Now, strolling through the campus, he felt like a fool. He held on tightly to his books. They felt like a security blanket, reliable and sturdy. He took out his cell phone and dialed home.

"Hello?" said Linda.

"Hey, Ma . . . It's just . . . me," said Jacob, a knot in his throat.

"Is everything okay, honey?" questioned Linda, surprised that Jacob had called this early in the morning.

"Actually, things are fine," Jacob replied. "I just wanted to tell you that I'm on my way to class. I know that I belong in school. Thanks for everything."

"Oh my, I'm so pleased you realize that, Jacob. I thank God for whatever it was that made you come to your senses. You know that Carl and I want what is best for you."

Jacob rolled his eyes. "Yeah, I'll come home this weekend so we can talk more about everything, especially Carl."

"Jacob, Carl knows, as a black man, how hard it is to not just make it, but to make it with something left over after the bills," she said. "He knows how important it is for you to be prepared in this world. And getting your degree still doesn't make the playing field even for you, but it at least allows you to not be at anyone's mercy."

"I know, I know, Ma," he said. "But sometimes you don't see everything. I'm at the arts building now, so I have to go. I'll see you this weekend."

"I love you, baby. Good-bye," said Linda.

Jacob flipped his cell phone closed.

He felt renewed in the secure and controlled environment the classroom offered. The professor was discussing John Locke and whether or not, when one mixed his labor with the land, if what he produced belonged to him. In other words, just because you make something, does it mean it is yours? One student said it depended on what you produced. He explained that if someone made a gun, then that person could use it to take away the property of someone else or something someone else had made. The discussion was lively. Jacob felt a letdown when it came to a close. He packed his books slowly, putting them in his knapsack and then leaving.

Since he had a couple of hours before his next class, he drove back to the apartment. As soon as he got to his room he began to study. He had a lot of work to make up for the time he'd missed. Before he could get deep into his books, LaJuan came in.

"What's up, man?" asked LaJuan exuberantly. "Come check out my new car. I've had my eye on it for a while. I didn't think it would still be there. But when I saw that it was, I bought it."

LaJuan was talking a mile a minute.

"LaJuan! LaJuan, listen!" Jacob raised his voice. "We need to talk."

"But my car. I really want you to see it," LaJuan said, trying to ignore Jacob's urgency. "Now I won't have to use yours."

"Nah, man, I ain't interested in seeing your car," Jacob said. "I can't even believe what you did to get it!"

Jacob tossed the book he was reading across the room, onto the bed, just grazing LaJuan.

"What are you talking about?" An incensed LaJuan threw his hands in the air.

"In Vegas I know you were having sex with them old-ass men," Jacob said, looking LaJuan straight in the face.

"Son, if it's any of your business, I had the money to buy that car before we left here," LaJuan retorted, attempting to avoid the real issue.

"So you let old men get up in your ass for a buck? How long you been rolling like this?" Jacob asked, now standing with his hands on his hips.

"Jacob, you a little rich, mama-pays-the-credit-card-bill boy! I don't expect you to understand," LaJuan said, heading out of the bedroom.

Jacob jumped in LaJuan's way. "I don't want no faggot room-mate!"

"I ain't no fag!" LaJuan said as he took a swing at his room-mate. Jacob dipped at the knees, dodging the blow.

"Now a sissy wants to fight?" Jacob balled up his fists and started dancing around the room like Muhammad Ali.

"Man, I'm not like you!" LaJuan said, raising his voice. "My family don't have no money! They're not paying my rent or my tuition. You don't see no care package come up in here like the kind your moms sends to you. I have to make it on my own, any way I can. I'm the first black man to ever go to college in my family—and I'm at Princeton no less!"

Jacob let his arms fall by his sides. "So why'd you drop out, then?"

"I didn't," he said somberly. "They kicked me out because I was behind on tuition. My financial aid covered only so much."

"But now you got enough cash to pay for school and you go out and buy a car?" Jacob said incredulously. "That's just ghetto. That's like living in the projects but driving a fancy car!"

"My intention was to reenroll, but I guess you could say it felt good to have some cash in my pockets and not have to worry about anything," he said. "I just got sick of not having shit. When I got that gig, I got to meet people like Juice. Yo, that dude is paid! After a while that poor shit gets real corny. Then I come home and see you getting a new fucking car for good grades. I get to take out another fucking loan. So if someone offered you money that you never, ever seen in your life, and finally you get to walk into a store and buy exactly what you want, and buy more than one of it, you would take it, too."

"You know what, I know this sounds like some preachy

bullshit, but after that weekend I believe what I'm saying," Jacob said. "If you stay in school, you'll have opportunities."

"Having cash gave me no worries," LaJuan repeated.

"Well, AIDS should be your number one worry," Jacob said matter-of-factly.

"I ain't got nothing to be concerned about," LaJuan said. "The senator ain't got no AIDS. He has a family. And it wasn't as bad as it sounds. Most times he just wanted to talk. One time he gave me a blow job. It was only the one time in Vegas that we did something serious."

"A senator? How do you know he's a senator?" Jacob asked.

"Like I said, sometimes we just talk."

"What about the other men? Who are they?"

"What other men? I haven't met any other men. My assignment was the senator only," confessed LaJuan.

"I saw Carl up in that joint!" Jacob said, chewing his nails.

"Get the fuck out of here! Not your stepfather? I've never seen anybody else with his mask off," LaJuan said. "Anyway, I'm not sure all those guys get down the way the senator does."

"How do you know that?"

"All I know is that it's a secret club. They gave me a card for access, but they take it away after each assignment is over," LaJuan said. "So you think Carl is on the down low? Are you going to tell your moms?"

"Of course I'm going to tell her. I have to."

"Don't you think you should talk to him first and find out what the deal is? What if you're wrong? That's going to tear your family down," LaJuan warned.

"Shut the fuck up! I know what I saw. Don't worry about what I need to do. You need to handle your own business, like figuring out where you're going to live, because you can't stay here—not as long as you're sticking with that group. I don't get down like that!"

Jacob collected his books and backpack and headed off to class.

"Man, you don't get it," said LaJuan, looking like he was going to cry. "You don't get out of this. That Bones dude don't take no for an answer. Here's how it works. He calls me, he tells me where to be, and I show up. If I don't show up, there's trouble. Real trouble, trust me."

"There's going to be real trouble if I come back and you're still here and still in that club," Jacob said before slamming the door. "I'm not living with a faggot here or back in New York!"

LaJuan pulled up to Club Eclipse; Bones was standing outside. Bones was anal about his business and he was making sure the security detail was in place and that the guest lists had all the names on them. LaJuan wouldn't have a few moments to collect his thoughts. He'd called for the meeting but was now very nervous.

"Nice ride, young blood," commented Bones as LaJuan got out. "Real nice. If I didn't know better, I would think you had your daddy's car!"

LaJuan gave Bones a pound with his chest puffed out ever so slightly.

"Thanks, man," LaJuan said. "I've been wanting a car for a long time. And I didn't want just any old hoopty, I wanted something hot. I still can't believe it belongs to me."

LaJuan stepped back to admire his car while he hit the alarm, then walked toward the entrance of Club Eclipse.

"Hold up," Bones said.

"What up?" asked LaJuan, eager to get inside to discuss his exit strategy.

"Well, you called me to have a meeting. What is it about?" Bones asked.

"Well, the thing is, I want out," LaJuan paused for a moment, waiting for a reaction from Bones. He didn't get one. Bones didn't even blink.

Feeling confident, LaJuan continued. "I got myself a car, which is what I really wanted. Now I think I can do the nerd thing and finish school and work my way up the corporate ladder."

"Okay," said Bones nonchalantly. "I'll check with the powers that be. Wait here."

LaJuan exhaled, relieved that Bones seemed unfazed. LaJuan smiled, impressed with himself.

Bones returned quickly.

"Juice is inside," he said. "He wants to speak with you. My advice to you, man, is just try and keep your talking down to a minimum."

"If you say so," said LaJuan.

Club Eclipse was gearing up for the evening crowd. Employees were taking chairs off the tabletops. Handymen were wiring the deejay's equipment. Juice and his driver sat in the back, at a booth.

"Hey, Juice, it's a pleasure formally meeting you," LaJuan said, holding out his hand to shake.

"Sit," Juice commanded, ignoring LaJuan's hand. "Let me start by saying you been making real good money, which means this is a real job, a real exclusive job that has treated you well. I know you got yourself a nice new ride. Don't you want to keep having nice things?"

"Yeah, of course. But I can find another way," replied LaJuan, feeling bold. "I don't want to do that shit no more. I don't know about you, but I'm not trying to have niggers park they dick in my ass for the rest of my life. I say if the shit happened to you once, it was an experience. But I ain't no fucking faggot. So if a man wants to keep getting fucked by men or wants to keep fucking men, then he's a faggot. Now, I can't take back what happened, but I'm not a sissy!"

Each time LaJuan said the word *faggot* it made Juice's jaws clench.

"Those are some strong words La," said Juice.

LaJuan, looking down at the table, was happy that he had a book of matches to play with to keep his hands busy.

"I don't like to judge people, you know. But I think that some people drink, some people smoke weed, and some people go to church." Juice spoke in calm, even tones. "Do you think that everyone who drinks is a drunk?"

LaJuan shook his head no.

"Do you think that everyone who smokes weed is a pothead?" asked Juice. "Well, I can answer the last one for you. Everyone who goes to church ain't a fucking Christian and I know people who have been going to church for years and they the fucking drunks and drug addicts. My point is that just because you're having sex with a man doesn't mean you're a faggot. It's just something that you like to do. Variety is the spice of life, they say."

Juice started laughing like a demon. LaJuan shifted in his seat and sweat gathered on his brow.

"I never thought about it like that," said LaJuan, scared and bringing it way down, and wishing he hadn't said any of the things he'd just said.

"I know," Juice replied. "And that's cool. But I need to know that you can keep quiet about what you've seen while working with us. Can you do that?"

"Hell, yeah!" LaJuan exclaimed, feeling more at ease. "There ain't nothing about my experience that I want to share with no-body. I'm taking that shit to my grave."

"Good. Then all this talk about business is over," Juice announced. "As far as I'm concerned, you and I are cool. As a matter of fact, the club is about to open in a couple of hours, so why don't you stay and chill in the VIP section and have some drinks on me. We can call it a good-bye party."

Juice patted LaJuan on the back and gave him a pound. LaJuan didn't want to stay, but somehow felt Juice's invitation was one that he couldn't refuse.

Juice then walked over to Bones, across the room examining the club's receipts.

"Does that motherfucker know how to keep his fucking mouth closed?" Juice asked through clenched teeth. "This ain't no shit that you just walk away from. How do I know that bitch ain't got a book deal or some other crazy shit? It's my job to protect the members of the Seven Figures and I need to know that he don't have any of my members on the news or on the front page of some tabloid!"

"He's a good kid," was all Bones would say. "He just wants to finish school and go on with his life. I don't think he has a plot to take you down."

But Juice wasn't totally convinced as he headed back to the booth to feel out LaJuan some more. During their conversation, LaJuan told Juice all he needed to know.

A bout thirty minutes later, a steady stream of people began to pour into Club Eclipse. The curtain came down in front of the VIP section; a waitress served Juice's favorite drink in tall glasses. Juice excused himself and returned a short while later with another waitress, carrying a tub of ice and more pre-opened bottles of expensive champagne.

"Drinks on me!" Juice yelled as the people in the other VIP booths got up and stood around Juice's booth. He took a bottle of champagne off the ice and handed it to LaJuan.

"To prosperity, people, to living the good life!" Juice yelled over the music and raised his bottle.

Everyone shouted and barked out, "To the good life!" as they toasted with Juice. LaJuan put the bottle to his lips and, responding to the crowd, he took a huge swig, trying to hold the bubbles in with the back of his hand.

"Hey, man, slow down," Juice warned. "That's some good shit there. You've got to sip it slowly."

It was too late, LaJuan had guzzled half the bottle, which was of some concern to Juice.

"You got to know when to say when, man," Juice abruptly said to LaJuan. "I think you should head home. You don't want to be pissy when you drive home in your new car."

"Good looking out," LaJuan replied. "And thanks for everything, Juice."

LaJuan slid out of the booth feeling like a new man, a burden off his shoulders. He made his way out of the club.

"Yo, LaJuan. Hold up," called Bones, who had to weave through the crowd to catch up with him. "How did it go?"

"Oh, it went real well. Thanks for everything, man. Juice was cool about it."

Bones followed LaJuan to his car. LaJuan rested against the automobile for a moment to regain his balance. He started to sweat. Feeling slightly light-headed, he closed his eyes momentarily and rubbed his hand over his face.

"You all right to drive?" Bones asked.

"Yeah, I just drank some champagne and my head's a little fuzzy," he said. 'I'll be fine once this night air hits me."

LaJuan let out an enormous burp, punching his chest.

"I feel better already," he announced.

Bones laughed as LaJuan got into his car and let the windows and the convertible roof down.

"Take care, man. I'm happy for you," Bones said, tapping the door of LaJuan's car to send him off. "Good luck. Keep in touch."

LaJuan flashed the peace sign and pulled out of his parking space. He turned onto Ninth Avenue, deciding to take the Holland Tunnel. It was closer than the Lincoln and the GWB. The stop-and-go traffic, even at this late hour, was making LaJuan's head swim. Just when he'd decided to pull over and wait, the traffic began to move. Once inside the Holland Tunnel, LaJuan turned on the air conditioner. He was sweating profusely. His arms and legs felt really heavy, especially his legs. It was as if he had done two hundred squats.

Once outside the tunnel, LaJuan decided against pulling over because there seemed to be cops at every turn and he wasn't sure he could pass that blood alcohol test. And besides, he was a black man in a shiny BMW.

Why did I have to guzzle that shit like that?

LaJuan decided to press on and sped up. The sooner he got

off the road, the better. The car was smooth, as if it was driving itself. He didn't even feel the speed climb quickly to over seventy-five. As he passed over the drawbridge on Route 1&9 between the Holland Tunnel and the turnpike, he suddenly felt all the strength go out of his arms. LaJuan could barely hold on to the steering wheel and found himself drifting into oncoming traffic. There was no divider on the drawbridge and there was no saving himself as a huge truck, heading north, was coming toward him full steam ahead. The truck driver had no option but to continue going straight. If he tried to avoid LaJuan's car, he would end up in the water.

Not only had LaJuan lost the strength in his arms, but he'd lost the feeling in his body from the chest down and wasn't able to step on the brake or change direction. He was a sitting duck. By the time he realized he would be a quadriplegic, it was too late. He never felt his legs crush and split open from the weight of the truck that had pounded through the front of his car. But he might have been able to survive that if only the impact of the SUV that hit him from behind, as he was spun back into his lane, hadn't snapped his neck.

LaJuan died instantly.

The antique Westminster grandfather clock almost blended into the wall even though it stood nearly six feet tall and had brass fixtures. It was made of Mortimer's favorite wood, mahogany, and had been shipped from England. Its chimes were not the loud, obnoxious gongs of other clocks. Its sound was softer, more musical.

Mortimer had summoned Juice to his penthouse. He had been watching Juice unravel over the last few months. Not just drunk with power, Juice seemed to have an all-out addiction to it. His new attitude made his protégé a lot less fun to be around, and Mortimer, with his eye on someone else, had become disinterested in spending time with Juice. Mortimer needed to have a man-to-man talk with Juice before things really got out of hand.

He wanted Juice to know that everything he had worked incredibly hard to achieve could be taken away in a flash if he wasn't careful. There were two dead bodies, two young boys, too close to Juice. The second death, LaJuan's, which at first appeared to have been an accident, had recently been discovered to be the result of foul play. It was murder, and the police were on the prowl, narrowing down suspects.

Mortimer didn't believe that Juice had had anything to do with either death, but what the man knew was that being that close to suspicious deaths was not good—especially given what they were planning for the future. If anyone took the time to connect the dots, they could be traced back to Juice. And Juice could lead to Mortimer—at the very least their association might be revealed. Mortimer had never welcomed attention and scandal, preferring that his life remain private. It was heat that neither Juice, nor the Seven Figures, needed. Mortimer had seen many a great start ruined like this.

He also wanted to talk with Juice about Brianna again. It was time for Juice to take a wife; there were advantages to being married. It showed the world that you were ready to move in certain social circles, and that you valued family—America's most important commodity.

Where Juice enjoyed a high-profile lifestyle, Mortimer didn't, which was why he didn't have to live by the same rules. Mortimer had always lived in the closet, and it suited his colorless personality.

"You need to have that, Juice," he had said. "You're not getting any younger and you need to have a steady woman on your arm. That playboy image gets tired after a while. Besides, the way we are playing this hand, you will be an adviser to the president of the Unites States one day. You have to have the right look."

Mortimer wanted to discuss a transition, too. He wanted to move on, to leave Juice totally in charge of the Seven Figures. But first he needed Juice to make him some promises. After that, he wanted to move on from their relationship. It was time.

Mortimer had been waiting more than an hour for Juice when he heard the private elevator come to life. Juice was the only one allowed to come up unannounced.

When the elevator opened, Mortimer led Juice to his bedroom. It was where so many of their deals, and plans, and dreams had unfolded.

Juice walked in behind him, not saying a word.

"Why so late?" Mortimer asked.

"I'm a busy man," Juice said, agitated.

"Do you know why I called you here?" Mortimer asked.

"What the fuck is this?" Juice exploded. "You sound like some fucking police officer when they pull you over. 'Do you know why I stopped you?' Cut the shit, Morty. Just tell me what you want to tell me. I have things to do!"

"You better watch your tone, boy," Mortimer said.

"Boy? Boy? Who the fuck do you think you're calling boy?" Juice spat out. "I ain't your motherfucking *boy!*"

"Well, you're acting like one!" Mortimer shot back. He rarely lost his temper. But he was incensed by the audacity of Juice's standing in his home—the home that had helped build everything Juice thought he wanted—and talking to him this way. It was too much. Mortimer took a few deep breaths and tried to collect himself.

"Look around you," Mortimer started. "Do you remember when you stood right here in this room and looked out at that view and I promised to give you everything you wanted? Remember that?"

"Oh, now you're going to throw all of that back in my face, huh?" Juice said. "You know why you did what you did. And you know why you're going to continue to do what you do."

Juice grabbed the thick hunk of member between his legs and Mortimer swallowed hard.

"You want this right now, don't you?" said Juice, moving closer to Mortimer, still holding himself through his cream-colored cashmere pants. Mortimer could see that Juice's penis was getting engorged.

"Tell me you want this dick, Morty," said Juice, coming up behind Mortimer, whispering in his ear as he pressed his hard penis against Mortimer's back.

This was the one thing Mortimer had a hard time resisting. Juice didn't wait for an answer. In one move, he had Mortimer bent over the black leather couch studded with brass buttons. In another move, he ripped down Mortimer's pants. The older man tried to put up some resistance, but it was halfhearted. He *did* want it. He wanted it *all*. When Juice rammed inside Mortimer with all his might, Mortimer let out a yell that seemed to come from the bottom of his feet. It was a mixture of excruciating pain and the most pleasure he had ever known.

Juice was talking to him throughout the whole attack.

"Scream louder, *boy!*" he said with another angry thrust. "Who's ass is this? Who's ass is this?"

Mortimer screamed louder, telling Juice exactly whose ass his ass belonged to. Juice reached around and stroked Mortimer as he pumped steady, even strokes into Mortimer's pliant behind. The sensation was too much for Mortimer and after a few minutes of Juice working him from both ends, he shot all over his couch, come spilling into the grooves of the brass buttons.

"You ain't done yet, boy!" Juice growled from behind as his

strokes became more rapid and ferocious. When Juice came, he pulled out of Mortimer.

"Milk me," he demanded. "Get it all!"

Mortimer took the semiflaccid penis into his mouth and sucked it dry. Juice leaned his head back and closed his eyes. Mortimer literally milked the little tremors away. When he was done, Juice didn't look at Mortimer. He headed for the shower without saying a word.

While Juice was in the steam shower, Mortimer sat at the end of his bed feeling weak and powerless, wondering how he was ever going to get Juice back on the right track.

"So is that what you wanted to talk to me about?" Juice said, toweling off as he walked over to the bed. "Because if you wanted some, all you had to do was ask. You know that. You didn't have to be all cryptic and shit."

Mortimer was silent for a moment, trying to shake off his sexual thoughts.

"I just want you to be careful," he said. "You've made a lot of enemies and you have a lot riding on the things you've put into play. Trust no one."

"Don't worry," Juice responded. "I've already put in place a plan to eliminate any enemies out there, even to protect me from friends who could become enemies simply from knowing too much."

"That's callous and reckless. What are you talking about? Who are you talking about? What kind of plan?" Mortimer had raised his voice in concern. He was convinced that Juice was even more out of control than he'd originally thought.

"Don't even worry yourself, Mortimer. I got this," replied Juice as if unaware of his friend's alarm.

The distance and coldness in Juice's voice sent shivers up

Mortimer's spine. He questioned whether he himself was one of those friends who knew too much. Would Juice actually turn on him one day? For the first time, he saw his lover as hollow and soulless. Mortimer quickly erased this assessment in his mind, unable to doubt his judgment.

"Also, I wanted to talk to you about Brianna."

"What about Brianna?" Juice asked, warming up a bit.

"I think you should make her an honest woman—and I don't mean with just getting married. I think you should do right by her."

"Well, you know if I do right by her, I won't be able to do right by you," Juice said, sliding onto the plush, king-size bed and massaging Mortimer's member.

"Stop," Mortimer protested, grabbing Juice's hand. "I know. This has to be it. What happened here today can't happen again."

Juice started laughing as he got up from the bed. He let the towel go, showing off his perfectly sculpted body. He stood there knowing that Mortimer couldn't take his eyes off him.

"I'm going to let you think about that one," Juice replied, slowly putting on his cashmere pants and shirt. "Because I don't think you mean it. But if it makes you feel any better, I have already considered marrying Brianna."

Juice believed that being married would make his stock rise. It would make him even more desirable, too. He realized that there was nothing sexier than a married man.

Mortimer was silent. Juice walked over to the edge of the bed and sat down next to his mentor.

"You worry too much," Juice said. "Everything will work out just the way I want it to. You'll see. I have to run, but you know I'm always here for you."

Juice leaned over and kissed Mortimer on the lips, then walked out.

Mortimer shook his head, trying to shake off Juice and all the thoughts—both painful and pleasurable—that he was having about him.

Juice and Brianna met at the Plaza Hotel in midtown for a late dinner. When Brianna approached the landmark hotel, she couldn't help being swept away by its beauty. The front looked like Prince Charming's palace in the Cinderella fairy tale. And she felt like the princess with the glass slipper. It was the Christmas holiday season and there were decorative lights everywhere; the horse-drawn carriages that lined Fifty-ninth Street were clopping around the hotel, adding to the ambience.

Accentuating the Christmas theme, the Plaza had wreaths hanging on every entrance, and a white candle had been lit in the window of each room. Outside, the bellhops and doormen were elegantly dressed in top hats, long-tailed coats, and red cummerbunds. They moved like mechanical toys as they assisted guests with their luggage. One of the doormen took Brianna's hand when she left her car and escorted her to the revolving doors, his white-gloved hand meeting her delicate one.

The dining room was lavishly decorated with floral wallpaper and matching carpeting. Juice, sipping a glass of wine, was waiting for Brianna. He immediately rose as Brianna approached the table.

"My love," he said as he kissed her hand.

"Oh, Lamar, you are just too much," she responded.

The chairs were well-cushioned, with high backs. Brianna melted into her seat. They enjoyed a fantastically long dinner, gazing into each other's eyes through five courses. By the time their tiramisu and coffee arrived, the romantic evening naturally led to the two lovebirds discussing Brianna's desire to settle down soon and have a family.

"I miss having my family around," she said.

Brianna explained that she'd grown up in the perfect home, with a loving mother and father. But something had happened when she was twelve, and no one would talk about it to this day.

"I came home from school and my daddy was gone," she said. "He never came back. My mother wouldn't tell me what happened. But whatever it was, it was serious. I loved my daddy, but it's hard for me to ever forgive him for leaving like that. I don't care what happened with my mother, he had no right to leave me."

Brianna started to tear up. It was a dark spot in an overall cheery disposition, something she never wore on the outside and worked hard to fix on the inside. But Juice appreciated getting to know this woman and it made him love her even more.

"He must have been out of his mind walking away from you," Juice said. "I don't know how any man could ever leave you."

Brianna went on to talk about how things had been tough for her mom, having to pull it together and take care of Brianna. But she more than managed, even springing for piano and singing lessons.

"I owe my mom a lot," Brianna said. "That's why I was so eager to make sure we took care of Mom-Mom, her mother. My mother was trying to take care of her by herself, but if you know anything about Alzheimer's, you'll know it's crazy and so, so sad. We now have her in a wonderful place and that burden isn't so much on my mother anymore."

"That was one of the things that made me fall in love with you," Juice confessed, "when you told me you were going to use your advance money to take care of your grandmother like that. It touched me."

"We have nothing if we don't have our family," she said.

That statement stung Juice as he thought of his own family, which consisted only of a mother he didn't speak to.

"What about your family?" Brianna asked the question Juice had dreaded most.

He kept up the lie of being orphaned before he was old enough to know anything and how he'd been raised in foster care and how he and Bones together had basically raised themselves and gotten through it. Brianna looked at him with sympathy and also admiration.

"You're living proof that you can get through anything and be somebody," she said.

Juice was unable to pull his eyes away from hers. He loved feeling this close to her but at the same time it scared him.

After dinner, the couple walked outside the Plaza and there waiting for them was a carriage pulled by a huge beautiful horse that looked like a Clydesdale.

"I was hoping you would want to take a ride," Juice said as he helped her into the carriage.

"I was eying them on my way into the Plaza," she said. "It's as if you were reading my mind."

They entered enchanting Central Park. Small streetlamps illuminated the road through the park and the reflection of the light, which hit the thin layer of snow on the grass, added a special glow. Brianna snuggled closer to Juice as she felt the chilly air. She leaned her head on his shoulder. They were about a quarter of a mile into the park when the carriage stopped in front of Tavern on the Green. The restaurant was lit up, and each tree outside was wrapped completely in tiny white lights, a beautiful spectacle.

Through the windows Brianna and Juice could see white-haired couples ballroom dancing. Enthralled by the dancers, Brianna was surprised when from out of nowhere a man in a tuxedo appeared, carrying a bouquet of a dozen white roses.

"For you, Ms. Banks," he announced and then disappeared into the darkness as the carriage continued on its journey.

"Oh, my goodness! For me? Lamar, you arranged this?" she exclaimed.

"Yes, I did. There's a small card attached," Juice said, smiling.

Brianna opened the card: *May you have a lifetime of friends.*

Brianna leaned over and gave Juice a passionate kiss. By this time, the carriage had come to a second stop. They were close to the ice-skating rink. There were people of all ages and various skill levels enjoying the ice. Juice and Brianna were both thrilled when they witnessed one of the skaters doing a triple axel, jumping high in the air and twirling three times before landing in a gliding stop.

It was about this time that another gentleman in a tuxedo approached the carriage. He was carrying two dozen yellow roses, which he set at Brianna's feet. She reached for the card: MAY YOU HAVE A LIFETIME OF HAPPINESS. Brianna beamed at Juice.

When the carriage came to a third stop, they were at the boathouse. A third man appeared, with three dozen red roses.

"'May you have a lifetime of love,'" Juice read out loud, along with Brianna, who was now aglow.

The park was sparkling and so was Brianna. Juice leaned close to his beautiful date who was smiling from ear to ear. He then pulled a Tiffany box out of the inside pocket of his cashmere coat.

"Will you make me the happiest man in the world?" he said, opening the box to reveal a seven-carat diamond. "Will you marry me?"

"I love you, Lamar. Yes, I will marry you."

The carriage, which more closely resembled a rolling bouquet because of Brianna's overflowing flowers, transported the engaged couple back to the Plaza, where Juice had booked them a room for the night. The following morning the two shared a lovely breakfast as they planned a spring wedding.

Bones had spent the last couple of nights tossing and turning. He'd been struggling with this feeling in the pit of his stomach ever since learning that LaJuan's death hadn't been an accident. It was undeniable that the finger of blame pointed squarely at Juice.

He is completely out of control!

Bones had done a lot of things on Juice's behalf that he wasn't proud of—some of them recently. But killing wasn't one of them. He had done it only once—a very long time ago—and it had haunted him ever since. And Benny had been a worthless, child-raping crackhead. But this boy had had a future. LaJuan and Lil Red, whose murder was becoming more and more clear to Bones, were just kids.

It was the visit from the detectives, giving him certain details of LaJuan's death, that helped him put two and two together. It looked as if he was on that suspects list and he didn't like it, didn't like any of it.

"So this young man was in your club right before driving off and getting killed?" the stocky red-haired detective asked. "And you have no idea how this drug got into his system?"

Bones answered honestly. He didn't know how a large dose of ketamine had gotten into LaJuan's system. It wasn't X or cocaine or 'ludes, recreational drugs. It was clear that someone had wanted to kill him. And the police were standing in Bones's condo, with their notepads, looking at him.

"You knew the young man. Did he have any enemies?" asked the other detective, a taller, well-built man. "Who would want to see him dead?"

Juice.

"I don't know," Bones answered. "He seemed well liked, just a nice kid."

"Um, before we leave, we have one more question: How well did you know Timothy Reddington, better known as Lil Red?" said the stocky redhead.

Bones could see it all playing out. Yes, it was a coincidence that he'd known both of these murder victims. But sometimes that was all the police needed to make a case. He knew they had more "evidence" than they were letting on.

Before they left, the tall detective handed his card to Bones.

"Please call us if you remember anything that might help us crack this case," said the man whose card read DETECTIVE MARK HALEY. "And please don't make any plans to leave the country; we might need to speak with you again."

It wasn't a request. It was official—Bones was a suspect.

After the two detectives left, Bones's mind was reeling.

"I guess what hasn't passed you hasn't caught you," he said aloud. It was one of the few words of wisdom he'd gotten from his mother. "Karma is a bitch!"

For most of his life, Bones had justified taking Benny's life. During the early years, he'd even felt good about it. It had fueled him, had given him a little extra boost as he walked the streets of Newark.

I killed a motherfucker! Don't fuck with me!

He walked around with a nasty confidence that inspired fear and respect. Nobody messed with Bones. But the ghost of Benny started to creep into his psyche as he began to read and mature and grow. As he began to value his life and his future, Benny's life took on more value. It shook him and it softened him.

And while he hadn't been arrested, or been made an official suspect in the murders of Lil Red and LaJuan, somewhere deep inside Andre Bonner was the feeling that perhaps he deserved to go to jail, that he deserved to pay. But he wasn't going to pay alone.

A couple of hours later, the doorbell rang. Bones looked puzzled. In the three years he'd lived there, he had never had any visits. Now there were two within a few hours.

He pushed the intercom.

"Who is it?"

"Yo, man, it's me, Juice! Let me up!"

Juice? Just the man I wanted to talk to. What a coincidence. So many coincidences.

Bones had been contemplating going to Juice's and confronting him. He was going to force him to confess to everything. He was going to get to the bottom of this, beat the truth out of him if he had to. He had spent the last couple of hours, after the police left, going over every detail. He wanted to make sure he had his facts straight. He had to be sure. He had to be ready to go down that road and not think about turning back. It could mean the end to everything. Bones was ready to walk away from the riches he had; he was ready to walk away from his friend.

The bell to his front door rang and Bones took a deep breath, then slowly walked to open it. His place was spare and simple, like him. It was a one-bedroom, all he needed, on the seventeenth floor. He liked living on the top floor; he didn't like people walking above him. When he looked out of his apartment, all he could see were the tops of trees and the open sky. On a clear day, he felt as if he were literally in the heavens and he liked that. His peace. His home. Bones didn't want that disturbed. He was going to get his peace back today.

He opened the door.

"My man!" Juice reached out to give Bones a big hug.

The man was beaming. Bones couldn't remember the last time, if ever, he had seen Juice this ebullient. Bones couldn't share in his happiness; his heart was too heavy. Juice was too into his own world to even notice.

"Yo! I have some *great* news! I asked Brianna to marry me last night and she told me yes!" said Juice, barely catching his breath. "I just left her and she wants to have a spring wedding and I can't believe it but I really want to do this. And I want you to stand up for me and be my best man!"

Bones waited and let Juice get it all out. Then he spoke.

"I would love to be your best man," he said. "If I can do it from behind bars. Because that's where I'll be, fucking with you!"

"What?" Juice's demeanor changed quickly. "What the fuck are you talking about?"

"I got a little visit today from two homicide detectives asking me questions about LaJuan and his *murder!*" Bones spat out. "And check this out: I just happened to be the one man who knows not just one murder victim, but two—they asked me about Lil Red, too! Now ain't that a bitch? And you know what I was thinking as I realized I was prime suspect number one? That I'm not the *only* motherfucker who knows something about this. Actually, I realized that I don't know shit!"

"Word? The cops were here?" Juice asked. "What did they ask you? What do they know?"

"Is that all you got to say?" Bones was on fire. "No, motherfucker! I'm asking the questions now. And if I don't get the answers I want, I will start talking about what I *do* know."

Juice was quiet. He walked to the black leather couch and sat down. He felt as though he had been sucker punched in the stomach. Bones walked over and stood in front of him.

"I need to know what you know, cuz," Bones said. "No more secrets. I'm not going to jail for some shit I didn't do. I need to know what's up. Your ass is rich and famous. Ain't nobody looking for you. They're coming for me and I'm not going out like that!"

"Come on now, man," said Juice, trying to calm Bones down. "You know I won't let you go out like that. I will get you the best lawyers money can buy."

Bones, now furious, pulled the mogul up by his collar so that they were eye to eye. Juice could see it all in Bones's eyes, all the anger. He knew he wasn't going to be able to talk his way out of this one, and that he couldn't throw money at this problem.

"I think you're missing the point here!" Bones was literally spitting his words into Juice's face. "I'm not *trying* to be defended. I'm not trying to be in no courtroom behind a wooden desk with some cracker whispering in my right ear about what he's going to say to the judge. That's *not* happening!"

Juice started sweating and stuttering.

"I-I-I got your back, Bones," he said. "I got this!"

"Tell me what went down with Lil Red and LaJuan," Bones said, not wanting to hear anything but the truth from Juice.

"They were both in the way," Juice finally conceded. "What I have been building . . . what I was trying to build, is bigger than I am. This is some shit like what the founding fathers did. This is about planning something now so that a hundred years from now ours will be taken care of. This shit is real big and I couldn't let no little bastards stand in the way. I had to clean up the mess."

"The mess! The mess?" Bones shouted. "You *made* the mess!"

"You better wake up!" Juice said, trying to be tough. "Look around you. How do you think you're living like this? I know what your bank account looks like even if you pretend to live low. I know where we came from. And getting here wasn't easy. We had to do a lot of things. We *both* had to do a lot of things to survive, to be on top. The seeds we're planting today will mean sowing so much power and freedom in the future."

"This has been your dream! I was just along for the ride, to cover your dumb ass," Bones said. "And who's the power for? You!"

"It's for all of us, cuz," Juice said. "Like I said, this thing is bigger than me. I'm sorry I've had to be so secretive, but I had to be. And I'm sorry you got caught up in all of this. I will make sure that you won't go down. I will do everything to make sure the heat is off you.

"Man, I love you like my brother. You were there for me the way my own mother never was. You saved my life from that fucking crackhead. When I wanted to die, you gave me something to live for. So I'm going to tell you now, on my life, this shit will be taken care of! You ain't got nothing to worry about."

Bones wanted to believe him. He wanted to look in Juice's eyes and see some truth. He needed to. Bones's anxiety level lessened a bit, and he was able to breath a little better.

"So, man, can we put all of that shit behind us and talk about some real serious business—my wedding!" Juice said, breaking into a smile and offering a pound.

Reluctantly, Bones returned the pound.

"Are you going to be my best man or what?" Juice said, his jovial spirit returning as quickly as it had left. "Will you stand up for me? It won't be right without my main man there by my side."

"I'll be there, man. I'll be there," Bones said, breaking into a slight smile.

"Good," Juice said. "I got a lot to handle, not just this wedding. I'll leave here and make sure this other shit is handled. Don't worry about a thing."

Juice straightened his sweater and gave Bones one more pound before letting himself out. As Juice closed the door, he realized that the only man who could send him down was the man on the other side of that door. Juice realized that Bones, too, would have to go.

Juice would call someone in Renard's firm to get the heat off Bones . . . for now. They couldn't secure a judge, but they had a few pawns in the police department they could throw off the scent—at least until the wedding was over. He didn't want anything to ruin that moment. His wedding had to be perfection.

But Bones was a problem. He knew too much. He knew way too much.

Chapter

29

Clearing out LaJuan's things was a tougher job than Jacob had imagined. LaJuan hadn't been just Jacob's roommate, he'd been his best friend. In the two years they'd known each other they'd had only one fight—on the day LaJuan had been killed.

Why did I have to be so hard on him?

Jacob carried a heavy burden of guilt. Since finding out that LaJuan's death hadn't been an accident, Jacob had started playing, over and over, the last words he'd said to LaJuan. He thought about how scared LaJuan had been, telling Jacob that if he tried to quit his new gig there would be trouble.

Why did I push him to quit, knowing there would be trouble? Why didn't I believe him?

Jacob loved LaJuan like the brother he'd never had. And he was going to miss him. As he carefully took LaJuan's things from his dresser, he tried to keep it as neat as it had been, while putting LaJuan's things in a canvas Ralph Lauren bag.

"I know it's not the Louis Vuitton luggage you wanted," Jacob said out loud.

LaJuan's things weren't just nice, they were coveted items. He had sweaters with leather patches, three-hundred-dollar jeans, Gucci loafers in two styles. He was meticulous about his appearance. His underwear drawer looked like something out of a department store, each pair folded perfectly and lined up in color order—whites to the right and colors to the left. Dividing his drawer, he had three colognes still in their boxes. He didn't mind if the scent of some of his favorite fragrances got on his underwear. His small closet was equally as impressive, with his shirts, jackets, and jeans occupying their own sections, shoes lined up underneath in perfect military order.

Jacob started to cry as he packed LaJuan's things. He couldn't imagine giving them away and he couldn't imagine keeping them. He was also sad because LaJuan had no one else to do what Jacob was doing. Jacob had learned more about his roommate in death. While LaJuan never talked much about his family and had never visited them the entire time he was in school, Jacob had no idea that he had no family.

LaJuan had grown up in the foster-care system. When the school called for his last known foster-care mother to collect his belongings, she told them that she couldn't come. She had other children, living children, who needed her attention. Jacob was left with the responsibility.

LaJuan's work desk was just as neat as his drawers and closet. Going through LaJuan's papers, Jacob discovered his school records. Every semester LaJuan was in school, he, too, had been on the dean's list.

I guess he deserved a car, too.

LaJuan played cool and tough and street-wise and acted like he wasn't really into that academic thing. But this desk told a different story. The most shocking find was a journal LaJuan had buried deep in the back of the desk drawer; next to the journal was a gun.

What the . . . ?

Jacob took the shiny firearm out of LaJuan's desk drawer, unwrapping it from a black T-shirt. He screwed the silencer on and off trying to determine if the gun had ever been used. Having never handled a gun before, Jacob couldn't tell. A strange excitement filled him, though, as he played with the gun. He was nervous and scared and thrilled.

He carefully concealed it in his backpack, then took the journal, which he decided he would read later. He loaded LaJuan's things into his car along with all his own belongings. Due to the death of his roommate, the school had released Jacob for the remainder of the school year with all A's to compensate for his loss.

On the ride to his parents', Jacob couldn't stop thinking about LaJuan, his death, that gun. He knew he'd left LaJuan in the apartment and had threatened him, telling him not to come back unless he quit that job. That crazy job. *Sex with a senator? What was he thinking?*

Could the senator have had LaJuan killed? Jacob had seen on television and in the news the underhanded dealings of politicians. He knew that some even had mob connections. He couldn't wait to read the journal; perhaps there would be some clues there, perhaps even the name of the senator. Jacob would get to the bottom of this. He felt he owed it to LaJuan to find his killer, especially since the last time he'd spoken to him it had been ugly. Jacob felt bad about calling him a faggot and leaving like that. He felt bad that their last words had been harsh.

As Jacob got closer to home, he turned over in his mind the problems there. Was LaJuan right? Should he give Carl a chance to explain himself before telling his mother what he'd seen in Vegas?

Jacob had a lot to think about during the hour-plus drive to New York. When he opened the door to their home, Carl was seemingly waiting for him. Carl wrapped his arms around Jacob and offered to go down with him and help bring up his things. Jacob's body responded with rigidity. His arms remained at his sides as Carl held him in a powerful, urgent embrace.

"I understand, son. I know you've been through a lot," was Carl's response to Jacob's silent coldness. "We can get through this together, as a family. Let me help you unload the car."

The two men worked in silence. There was only the *plunk!* sound of the bags hitting the curb. The doorman watched the bags as Carl and Jacob took as much as each man could carry in separate trips upstairs. Jacob engineered their assembly-line routine of unloading the car so that while Carl was going up in one elevator, Jacob was coming down in another. Jacob didn't want to be in such tight quarters with Carl. He was disgusted by the man. Throughout the whole process, the gun concealed in the backpack on his shoulders gave him comfort.

By the time they came up with the last load, Linda, who had been taking a nap, was there at the door. She ran up to Jacob, passing her hands all over his face and then down to his shoulders as if making sure that all his body parts were there.

"Jakey, I love you," she said, tears running down her face.

She kissed Jacob on the cheek and wrapped her arms around

him. Jacob hugged her back. It felt good to hug his mother and melt in her unconditional love.

"I'm so glad you're home," she said. "Baby, I'm so glad you're here."

"I love you, too, Mommy." Tears welled up in Jacob's eyes and he felt like an eight-year-old again. He wanted to curl up and let his mommy take care of everything.

In the background, Carl marched back and forth between the foyer and Jacob's room delivering bags.

Linda stood back and examined her son from head to toe.

"Carl is glad to have you home, too," she said. "He has taken the whole day off from work to be here for you."

Jacob rolled his eyes, which Linda missed because she was too busy hugging him and fussing over him. She guided her son into the living room. A fire was burning in the fireplace, which added to the coziness of home. It wasn't that cold, despite its being winter, but the fire created an atmosphere that Jacob had grown to love over the years. It was one of his favorite features of their home. He joined his mother on the couch, letting the backpack rest at his feet.

"Jacob, I am so sorry for what happened to your friend," Linda said, extending her condolences. "I can't believe all this has happened, especially when I was thinking that things had finally calmed down around here, with you going back to school and everything."

"Yeah, Mom, I can barely believe that LaJuan is dead," he said.

"Can you imagine anybody who would want to kill him?"

"Yeah, can you?" asked Carl, butting in on his way to deposit the last of the bags in Jacob's room. "We can't let them get away with this."

Jacob turned his attention directly to his mother, making it clear to Carl with his body language that this was an A and B conversation and he should C his way out of it.

"Ma, I don't even know," said Jacob, placing his head in his hands.

"I've been so frightened for you, ever since they reported that LaJuan had drugs in his system," said Linda, whose hands were shaking. "Son, you can tell me. You guys weren't up at school using drugs, were you?"

"Of course not, Mom! Neither of us used drugs. We smoked a few blunts while we were hanging out sometimes, but nothing serious. Nothing hard-core. And the stuff they found in his body wasn't recreational. Somebody was *trying* to kill him."

Linda wanted to admonish him for smoking blunts, but decided that it wasn't important enough nor was it the right time. She would have that "Just say no" discussion with him another time.

"Mom, I just want to go lie down," Jacob said, drained from the death, the drive, and the drama surrounding LaJuan. "This has all been too much for me."

He rose to his feet and picked up his backpack.

"Oh, baby, I understand. Go get some rest."

Jacob crossed Carl's path in the long corridor that led to his bedroom.

"Jacob, thank Carl for helping you with all those bags," Linda hollered down the hall.

Jacob stared coldly at Carl. He forced a stingy "Thanks!" out of his mouth while his eyes glared at Carl.

"Noooo . . . problem . . . man," Carl said, placing his hand on Jacob's arm. He could feel the chill but couldn't quite understand the source.

Jacob shoved Carl's hand off his arm and continued swiftly to his room. Carl's eyes followed Jacob down the hallway and he chalked the weird behavior up to stress.

The next day, at about eleven in the morning, Linda was up and ready to go out. She had a few errands to run but didn't want to leave the house before Jacob was up. Earlier she had made him breakfast, but it was still on the stove. Sitting in the kitchen, she started to shuffle through the mail. They had received an invitation. She opened up the lovely Jamie Ostrow–designed package.

"Carl, we have a wedding invitation," said Linda as she placed the rest of the mail on a table in the foyer. "We are cordially invited to the union of James Lamar Kennedy and Brianna Banks. I think Jacob will enjoy seeing all those celebrities. Maybe it will help."

"When is it?" Carl asked.

"Oh, not until the spring."

"Well, it will give us something to look forward to. There won't be just celebrities there. That Kennedy fellow has a lot of friends in high places."

"I bet he does," replied Linda. "I'm just looking forward to getting a nice dress and looking glamorous. We haven't been out on the town like that in a while. I can't wait."

Carl gave Linda a smile and nodded his approval.

"Hon, I'm not sure when Jacob is going to get up and I don't want to disturb him. He's been through so much," Linda said. "I'm going out to get some air and take a few Christmas gifts to the post office. I'll be back shortly. Will you check on him periodically?"

Carl agreed and Linda gave him a peck on the cheek as she collected her purse and left.

Carl instantly wiped the smile off his face. He was sitting at the island in the kitchen with a cup of coffee before him. He was thinking about Jacob's rude behavior, perplexed. While the two had never been close-close, Carl realized that Jacob had been acting really strange since he'd returned home yesterday. *What an ungrateful little bastard.*

He thought about the last time he'd spent quality time with Jacob, at the basketball game last spring. It wasn't long before he began to think about LaJuan, and LaJuan's connection to Bones, and then Bones's connection to Juice. He wondered if it was worth having a conversation with Bones. He immediately dismissed the idea of doing so. It would appear strange, he reasoned, as Bones was not on his level nor had they ever had much interaction.

"What in the world are the odds of Jacob's being caught up in my business?" said Carl out loud, much to his surprise.

"What did you say, Carl?" asked Linda, who had just returned. She hadn't been gone long but she returned to find Carl in the exact same position she'd left him in, with a cold, untouched-up cup of coffee in front of him. The *Wall Street Journal*, on the table, remained neatly folded. Carl had been sitting at the counter deep in thought for quite some time without realizing it.

"Oh, nothing, Linda," he replied. "I'm just thinking about Jacob and everything. That's all."

"I know," she said. "The truth is, I've never seen him so . . . I can't put my finger on it. He seems more angry than anything else. I hope he'll come around in a few days."

"I'm sure that he will." Carl placed his hands on Linda's

shoulders. "I'm going to go to my study and get some work done," he said, kissing her on the cheek.

When Carl turned around, he saw Jacob, fully dressed and with his backpack on his shoulder. The young man caught Carl's eye and glared at him. Carl hesitated a moment, then passed by Jacob, saying, "Good afternoon, son." Jacob didn't say a word.

Carl walked down to his office and locked the door behind him. He dialed Mortimer from his special iPhone.

"Mortimer, it's Carl," he said.

"Ahh, Carl. How are you, my friend?" greeted Mortimer.

"Not good," he said, releasing a breath. "What are the chances that Juice . . . that *we* would hire a boy-toy who just happened to be my son's roommate?" Carl still couldn't believe the insanity of it all.

"You know what they say about six degrees of separation between us all," Mortimer replied.

"Well, you just need to know that I'm living with a live grenade," Carl said. "And I don't know when that pin is going to be pulled. I don't know how much Jacob knows about my involvement with Seven Figures. I don't know what his roommate might have told him. I could lose everything I've built with Linda if he decides to open his mouth to his mother. She would not approve of my belonging to a secret club, especially one that costs a million dollars a year. I have no power and no control with Jacob knowing I'm a member."

"You always have control, and sometimes you have to look for power, but it's usually right under your nose," Mortimer responded.

Carl looked at the phone. Stressed, he wasn't in the mood for Mortimer's riddles.

"What are you talking about, Mortimer?" asked Carl, a scowl on his face.

"Well, you just need to have something on your boy of equal value," stated Mortimer.

"Like what?" Carl questioned. "He's a freaking teenager who's been sheltered his whole life! What do I say: I know you sneaked into a bar and got drunk?"

"Settle down, Carl," Mortimer said. "I don't think the boy is going to say much of anything. First of all, if Jacob knows anything, he must know it firsthand."

"What do you mean?" asked Carl, wishing that the old man would get straight to the point.

"Jacob was with LaJuan in Las Vegas," Mortimer started. "And I have it on good authority that he spent the night in the company of Xavier Prince. So whatever he does know, he will have to fess up to what he's been up to also."

Carl started laughing. He couldn't believe Mortimer's words. There was no way they could be true. He had known Jacob most of the boy's life and there was absolutely no indication that he would spend an evening with a man. In fact, he seemed completely naive about the gay lifestyle. Carl couldn't even recall Jacob ever mentioning or commenting on a gay man—negatively or positively. Jacob didn't even seem aware of homosexuality.

"So you're telling me that Jacob was in Vegas?" said Carl.

"That's what I'm saying," announced Mortimer.

Carl grew angrier and angrier by the second. He searched frantically in his bills drawer looking for Jacob's credit card bill. He was stunned to discover that Jacob had charged a dinner at the Bellagio on the same weekend he'd been there.

"Wait a minute!" he said.

"Look, LaJuan brought your son in on this," Mortimer said. "I don't think Juice knew that Jacob was your stepson."

"Well, that's no consolation," Carl replied.

"Don't worry, old friend. It will all work out. I'll speak with you later," said Mortimer. "There is something I need you to do. I'll give you a call in a few weeks."

On his way out, Jacob passed Carl's office. He was distracted by the loud talk and he stopped and pressed his ear against the door to listen. When the conversation was over, Jacob tiptoed away from the door.

Yeah, I was in Vegas and I know EVERYTHING, you fucking homo.

Jacob had heard about men on the down low, but he'd never thought he would have to face such a thing in his own life. Here he was living with this man who had practically raised him as his own, this man his mother loved, and who was on the down low. This man was pretending to be a devoted husband and father while living out his fantasy with men.

Jacob arrived at Bones's apartment. He'd gotten the address from LaJuan's diary, which had everything he had been doing written in very neat, very organized, very thorough notes with dates, full names, locations—everything.

He rang Bones's bell.

"You've got to be kidding," Bones said out loud as he went to the intercom to find out who was here to visit him now. Three visitors in one day almost sent him over the edge.

Bones buzzed Jacob up.

"Man, what are you doing here?" asked Bones as he opened the door to let Jacob in.

"I won't take up much of your time, but I need some answers."

"Yeah, everybody seems to need some answers these days," Bones replied.

"Do you know who killed LaJuan?" Jacob asked, looking at Bones accusingly and getting right to the point of his visit.

"Whoa, homey," Bones said. "Let me just be clear. I liked the lil dude. When he came to me, wanting out, I gave him my blessing. I thought everything was cool. I had no reason to see him dead."

"So who killed him!" Jacob screamed. "Who the fuck killed him!"

Bones could see how torn up Jacob was and he felt for him. He stood there quietly, with a somber look on his face. Jacob knew that Bones knew something and he couldn't take it. He started pushing and grabbing Bones.

"Tell me who did it! Tell me who did it!"

Bones wrapped Jacob in his powerful arms.

"Slow down, man," Bones said. "Calm the fuck down before you get hurt. Like I told you, I didn't do it!"

"But you know who did!" Jacob said.

"I can't say for sure that I know who killed LaJuan. But maybe he knew too much and maybe he made some people uncomfortable. You have to follow the money. Who would profit most from LaJuan's death?"

"Was it the senator?"

Oh shit! He knows about the senator! Normally Bones would store that information and run to Juice with it. But he didn't want another dead young body to turn up. He could also see that Jacob was determined. He would get himself hurt if he kept going around recklessly asking questions like this. Bones had to give him something to slow him down.

"No, it definitely wasn't the senator," he said.

"So you do know," Jacob said, looking at Bones. "Who was it?"

"I can't say," Bones said.

"If you don't say something, I'm going to the police."

Not them again!

"You're a smart kid," Bones said. "I know you can figure it out."

"Was it that stupid faggot group? Was it Juice? Did he do it?" Bones was silent. He walked to his door and opened it, his head down in shame. Jacob had his answer and he walked out. He was still angry but at least now he had some satisfaction. He didn't know what he was going to do with the knowledge. Bones was relieved. If Juice didn't handle the situation, it would be handled for him. Maybe this boy would go to the police and it would all be over.

T he apartment was dark and quiet when Jacob reached home. He wasn't sure if anyone was there. He turned on the light at the door.

"Hey, Jacob," Carl said. He was sitting on the couch, in the dark, a glass of scotch on the rocks in his hand.

Jacob, not wanting to make eye contact with Carl, picked up the wedding invitation, sitting on the table in the hallway.

"Oh yeah, your mother got that today," Carl said. "She's looking forward to it and thought you would enjoy it, too. It's probably the hottest ticket in town. That Brianna is all over television and everywhere else. You're a lucky kid to be attending the wedding of two mega stars like Juice and Brianna."

"Yeah, real lucky," replied Jacob sarcastically.

"Son, come over here a minute," ordered Carl. "I want to talk with you."

Jacob lowered his backpack and let it rest on the floor in the foyer. He walked farther into the living room. Carl motioned for him to sit down. The serious look in Carl's eyes was not one that Jacob had seen before. It made him uncomfortable. Somehow, in Jacob's mind, it seemed that Carl had the upper hand, but that couldn't possibly be the case. Jacob held up his finger to Carl. He returned to the hallway, then came back with his back-pack. He sat in the chair facing Carl. He placed his backpack down at his feet.

"Jacob, is there something you want to talk to me about?" asked Carl.

"No," said Jacob, chewing on his fingernails. "Is there something you want to talk to me about?"

Not interested in playing kids' games, Carl stated without emotion, "Jacob, I understand that you were in Vegas a few weeks ago."

"Yeah, I was and so were you," said Jacob sarcastically.

"Yes, I was there on business—and you?"

"I went with LaJuan and I saw you there."

"You did? Why didn't you say something to me?" asked Carl, surprised.

"You were too busy," Jacob said, leaning forward in the chair, his eyes glaring at Carl.

"How could I ever be too busy?" Carl asked, confused.

Jacob stood up, and raising his voice, he spit out his words through clenched teeth. "You were too busy getting plugged in the ass!"

Carl rose to his feet, now standing face-to-face with Jacob. He pulled his arm back as if winding up for a fast pitch and jabbed his finger in Jacob's face, half an inch from his nose.

"How on earth could you say something like that to me?" Carl protested. "You're the one who was with Xavier."

"I wasn't with nobody!" Jacob knocked Carl's hand down, out of his face.

Carl brought it back up and pointed again.

"Look, you are never to raise your voice to me again," Carl said, attempting to regain some kind of control. "And you definitely are not going to touch me in such a disrespectful manner ever again! Do you hear me, young man?"

Carl's eyes pierced through Jacob.

"I know my mom would want to hear what I saw you doing in Vegas," Jacob said, not backing down in the least.

"You didn't see me doing anything!" Carl still protested. "I wouldn't tell your mother any craziness like that if I were you."

"There's no way I'm going to let my mother stay married to a homo," Jacob shot back.

"Man, you're crazy," Carl said. "You didn't see me doing shit!" Carl never cursed, but he was losing control.

"I saw your brand on your leg. Man, I know what you look like, even with a mask on! I saw the whole thing!"

The room was silent. Carl's mouth hung open, his eyes wide. Jacob sat down and put his backpack on his lap. Carl sat down on the couch slowly. His eyes were fixed on the ceiling.

"You must have seen Renard's, my frat brother's branding, 'cause I know it wasn't me," said Carl, trying anything to get out of this.

"No, it was you!" Jacob said, clenching his backpack and leaving the room.

He stomped down the hallway to his bedroom, his mind swirling with the information from his conversation with Bones and his argument with Carl. *Carl is out of control. What kind of denial trip is he on? I know what I saw. And this Juice guy is a monster! He has to be dealt with.*

Just then, Jacob had an idea. He wanted to run to the police with the information he had, but he was certain that Juice was rich enough and powerful enough to get away with the murder. He had watched money get people out of a lot of messes. And he had no support. Carl could help, but there was no way that he would. He was too deep in the mess himself. It was clear to Jacob that he would deny everything and would help Juice. No, Jacob had to handle this on his own. He was pissed because he would have to wait. But the wait would give him time to plan it all and be certain.

"Yep, I'll be at that wedding, all right," he said. "I wouldn't miss it for the world."

Jacob retreated to his room. He locked his door, placed the backpack next to his bed, and turned his music up loud. He was rocking to Nas's *Illmatic* CD, a classic. He was rapping along with the master, and the music took him to another place. He forgot all of his worries and got up and started dancing. He took the gun out of the bag and waved it around as if he was starring in a Western. For a moment he was in a trance. For a moment he felt powerful. For a moment he felt that everything was going to be just fine.

It was Friday evening, and Audrey and Xavier were at the Metropolitan Museum of Art, sitting at one of the small tables on the balcony overlooking the main lobby. There was a buzz of excitement as tourists and city dwellers were eager to begin their stroll through one of the world's most renowned museums. The couple was listening to a live pianist, flutist, and violinist perform Beethoven. They were enjoying wine and cheese, and an intimate conversation, as they privately celebrated Xavier's big career move.

"Audrey, you'll be invited to every game," he said. "You could come to the owner's suite and watch the game there. Or I could get you courtside seats, whatever you want."

Xavier noticed that Audrey's eyes were beaming, listening to him brag about one of the small benefits of owning an NBA team.

"I think that would mean flying me to Vegas all the time," said Audrey. "I really don't think my hair could take that."

They both laughed as Audrey pretended to be adjusting a wig.

"Your company is opening that branch in Las Vegas. Would you consider transferring out there?"

"Xavier, I would have to give that some thought—even if my company would consider it. But I have to be honest. I would have to have a reason, a commitment, to uproot myself and my life."

"Any woman would. And you deserve that," Xavier replied, realizing that the gleam in Audrey's eyes had disappeared even though she was looking directly at him. His mind wandered back to Marcello's wife. In that moment he knew that he desired the same adoration in a wife. Suddenly, the museum didn't have its same magic, but Xavier continued nonetheless. "Audrey, would you do me the honor of attending Juice's wedding with me?"

"Of course. I have read everywhere that he's getting married to his artist Brianna Banks. Her songs are on the radio all the time. This will be the social event of the year," Audrey said, the gleam returning to her eyes.

SPRING, PRESENT DAY
New York City

James Lamar Kennedy, known to the world as Juice, stood at the altar in his white silk Armani tuxedo, a stark contrast against his chocolate skin. Television cameras and crews were set up near the front of the altar. Bright lights were everywhere. Competing with the confusion was the harpist, playing Bach's "Be Thou with Me."

The church was packed with movie stars, athletes, and businessmen, the pews full. However, the first row was reserved for family. Since Juice didn't have any family members present, it was filled with friends he considered family—or at least at some point had.

Juice looked out into the audience. Mortimer was in the very back, discreetly in the corner, handsomely dressed in a tan Hugo Boss suit. No one would notice him, except Juice.

There were other moguls and movie stars peppered throughout the church. Toward the front was Xavier Prince, NBA team owner. Sitting next to him was Audrey, running her fingers through her hair, enticing Xavier with its scent. Xavier, in a gray silk-and-wool suit was still grinning from ear to ear, thinking about his latest accomplishment. He winked at Juice.

Next to them were Carl, Linda, and Jacob. Jacob had spent the last few months in his room, unresponsive. This was one of the first times he'd been out of the house and Carl and Linda were happy. His mood seemed to have turned around.

"Hey, Aunt A," he said, sliding in next to her and giving her a warm kiss.

Audrey kissed him back and smiled. She had been worried about him, too. It was good to see him. He looked so handsome.

As the guests got settled, the harpist moved her hand away from her instrument. Brian McKnight took the floor, sitting behind the piano and singing "Love of My Life." At the end of Brian's song, the processional lined up to make their entrance. A bridesmaid appeared in the doorway then walked to the front of the church. Three more bridesmaids followed, wearing matching cream-colored lace dresses.

The maid of honor entered the church, also wearing a cream-colored outfit, in a different style from the others. Behind her was the ring bearer. The little four-year-old boy looked adorable in his jacket with its long tails. He was carrying a purple velvet pillow.

The ushers rolled out the white carpeting. Simultaneously, six white doves were released from their cages, located around the pews. The birds circulated through the room, trailing large lace ribbons spun with gold. A little girl carrying a basket of purple violets and white roses sprinkled them along the aisle as she slowly walked toward the front of the church.

Brianna Banks stood at the back of the sanctuary, prepared to walk down the aisle. She wasn't quite sure how she had gotten there. The past few days had been a bit of a blur. She imagined that the butterflies in her stomach must have carried her, because they were raging in her belly.

Butterflies or not, Brianna looked like an angel in her antique white gown with the thirty-five-foot train. Her gown had been flown in from Italy, with more than thirty carats' worth of diamonds sewn into the bodice. It had cost $350,000. No expense would be spared for this wedding, Juice had insisted when the price came up. Brianna had decided that after the wedding, she would turn those jewels into earrings for her seven bridesmaids and cuff links for the groomsmen.

The harpist played the wedding march, cueing Brianna to begin her procession down the aisle. Her mother escorted her. It was a break from tradition, but Brianna couldn't think of another person she would have give her away on this special day. When she suggested it to Juice, he didn't hesitate.

"That woman has been more of a father to you than any man you could have stand next you," he told her. "I demand it. Besides, I think it will be dope to see two beautiful women coming down the aisle like that on my wedding day."

Her mother wore a royal purple gown with sequins. It was clear who Brianna had gotten her looks from as the two walked down the aisle as choreographed. But all eyes were on Brianna. Her train spanned out perfectly along the white silk runner with the white rose petals sprinkled everywhere. Oohs and ahs were audible as all in the church rose to their feet to catch a glimpse of the bride. Brianna was captivating—more beautiful than Princess Di when she'd married Prince Charles.

The veil was intricate and masked her face, hiding the tears of joy that began to stream down as she focused on her groom, looking handsomer than she could ever have imagined. Brianna took a deep breath, inhaling the scent of fresh flowers and expensive perfume. She could see her man, and her nerves were immediately calmed. Brianna had never been more sure about anything and she couldn't wait to get down that aisle to say "I do!"

She was tired of being on tour; she was tired of the movie sets. She was tired of being a sex symbol. She was tired of being a singer. She was tired of being an actress. She was tired of being Brianna Banks. She wanted to settle down and be Mrs. James Lamar Kennedy, have a couple of kids, and be "normal."

The last few years had been anything but normal. She'd gone from playing clubs and showcases to becoming the most popular and sought-after face in America. She'd capped that with a whirlwind romance with one of the most recognized and famous names in entertainment. Everywhere they went they encountered paparazzi and autograph seekers. It seemed that everyone wanted a piece of them. They couldn't take a simple stroll in the park or grab a hot dog at Gray's Papaya the way she had in the old days.

As Brianna got close to the altar, she knew her life would never be that kind of normal again. But she was willing to forsake that for what was in front of her: *Juice.*

She stood at the altar and her Lamar took her hand in his strong, steady grasp; she knew that this was real, that she was finally about to *live* her life. Live her life with him.

The two of them looked like the negatives to the little white bride and groom on top of the wedding cake. Bishop Howard, the officiator, waited for the music to stop before he began. He was one of the most respected men of the cloth in the country and the mentor to Seven Figures member Rex Longfellow.

"Dearly beloved, we are gathered here today to join this man and this woman . . . ," Bishop Howard began.

Juice and Brianna had written their own vows. Brianna watched Juice say his and was turned on by his full lips. She started daydreaming about what they would be doing after the wedding, on their honeymoon. He told her he had a surprise for her and she was looking forward to it; she liked Juice's surprises. So much had been going on over the last few months, releasing an album, going on tour, preparing for this wedding, that they hadn't had much time together. Her body ached for him.

Sitting toward the middle of the church, Jacob couldn't keep still. His palms were sweating and his heart was racing a mile a minute. Being this close to Juice was making his skin itch from the inside out. He wanted to scream but sat there beside his mother, two seats away from Carl.

The ceremony was winding down. Bishop Howard had gotten to the part right before pronouncing Juice and Brianna husband and wife.

"If anyone present can show just cause as to why this couple may not be legally joined together . . . ," Bishop Howard said.

A long silence ripped through the church as a few looked around and some even giggled.

Juice chuckled to himself and wondered if he had ever even heard of anyone actually stopping a wedding. Sure, he had seen it plenty of times in the movies and on television, but never in real life. He turned and eyeballed the crowd, saying, "All right, now!" which caused the church to erupt in laughter. Bishop Howard cleared his throat as a signal to settle down.

Jacob sat in his pew sandwiched between his mother and Audrey. His left leg began to shake and fear pulsed through his body, pure fear. He was sure that it had a scent and that he reeked of it. Jacob focused on an elegant white calla lily that had landed near his left foot. The church was filled with thousands of them. Jacob held tightly to the back of the pew, forcing his mother to give him a curious glance. But he needed all the support he could gather as he made his way to his feet.

"By the power . . . ," Bishop Howard said, continuing the ceremony.

"Wait!" Jacob shouted, cutting off Bishop Howard. "I can't let this go on!"

The crowd erupted in grumbles and mumbles and confusion.

"That man is a faggot and he killed my roommate!" Jacob shouted, reaching in his waistband and pulling out the gun.

Bang! Bang! Bang!

Pandemonium broke out as people started running for the exits. Xavier grabbed Audrey by the hand and pulled her to the floor and the two crawled out of the church, trying to avoid the crush of people heading out and now also into the church in their direction. They passed the two beefy bodyguards who had been stationed discreetly at the back of the church and who had now tackled Jacob so hard that all of the wind had been knocked from his body. They wrestled the gun from his hand and pinned him on his stomach, stretching his arms behind him, a knee in his back. There were already police just outside, so within minutes Jacob seemed to have most of the force on his back. Handcuffs, kicks, and punches followed.

Linda, being pulled by Carl, let out a blood-curdling scream, a helpless scream, as she managed to make sense of what was going on all around her. She couldn't believe that her baby was being brutalized, and secondary to that thought was that her baby had put two bullets into Juice Kennedy. One bullet had sailed just over the bishop's head, breaking a stained-glass window at the side of the church.

It wasn't bad work for Jacob, who had never handled a gun before. But as he lay on the hard church floor, one eye shut from punches and blood spilling from his mouth, he began to realize what he'd done. And thoughts of jail for the rest of his life entered his mind.

While he'd planned and thought about this shooting for a couple of months, he hadn't thought about what would happen after it. He was so consumed with revenge that he paid no attention to the very real prospect of arrest and court dates, trials and prison.

As the church cleared out, Carl had to hold Linda back, scooping her up in his arms and carrying her away from the scene.

"Don't worry, baby," he whispered in her ear. "I'm going to get Jacob out of this. Don't worry."

Carl managed to carry Linda outside the church, where he grabbed his special iPhone and made a call. Everyone he needed was in the church, but in the mayhem they had all scattered. Even though Carl had whispered those words of comfort in Linda's ear, there was no way he could imagine getting Jacob out of this one. He'd shot a man in public, with three hundred witnesses and millions more viewing on television screens around the world. There would be no mistaken identity with this. He needed to get hold of Renard and then Mortimer. Together they would know what to do.

Screams and sobs could be heard from inside the church. Brianna Banks, her veil now flipped back over her head—an act her husband should have performed—was on the floor over Juice's body. She was hysterical.

"Why! Why! Why!" she screamed with that voice crafted in heaven, so loud and so powerful and now so sad.

The ambulance had arrived just as quickly as the police. Bones and her mother jumped into action, trying to soothe her, to calm her, but Brianna could not be consoled. She clawed at the men lifting Juice's body onto the stretcher as Bones tried to hold her back. She was determined to ride in the ambulance with him.

"Brianna, no," Bones said. "Let them do their job."

"I'm going with my husband!" she managed through heaves and sobs. "I'm not leaving him!"

Her mother gave Bones a look that told him he would be wasting his time to try to convince her not to go. She was determined.

Brianna climbed into the back of the ambulance, trying to gather up her thirty-five-foot-long train. It had several hooks in the back that would release it, leaving her with a sleek dress that she had planned to show off at the reception. She didn't have time to look for the hooks and fumble with them. So she grabbed a pair of scissors from the tray inside the ambulance and frantically cut away the expensive train, leaving it on that New York City street.

Brianna grabbed the hand of the man she loved as the paramedics worked on him feverishly, injecting him, filling him with tubes and pumps to make him breathe artificially because he wasn't breathing on his own.

James Lamar Kennedy lay on this stretcher contemplating death, this time his own. As the life drained from his body, he could feel the squeezes on his hand, could hear the muffled cries and pleas to "Hang in there, baby. Don't leave me!"

He didn't want to leave. He was going to fight to stay.

Printed in the United States
By Bookmasters